CW00520515

LEAH

Elisabeth Price

MINERVA PRESS

ATLANTA LONDON SYDNEY

LEAH
Copyright © Elisabeth Price 1998

ISBN 0 75410 284 X

First Published 1998 by
MINERVA PRESS
Sixth Floor
Canberra House
315–317 Regent Street
London W1R 7YB

Printed in Great Britain for Minerva Press

LEAH

The Hall

Leah lay supine in the feather bed, enjoying a straggling beam of sunshine filtering through the grimy skylight high up in the attic of the great house. Beside her, Lizzie snored gently, her arms above her head in complete relaxation. With a grimace of distaste, Leah thrust back the crocheted bedspread and carefully put her feet to the bare boards. The iron bedstead creaked warningly; Leah stood still in a shaft of sunlight. She was tall and slim, her limbs long and shapely, the fragile build disguising her strength. She was not beautiful, her features were too irregular for that, but there was a compelling vulnerability about her face. She had large grey eyes, shaped by black eyelashes, which dominated her face, and a childishly endearing nose tilted above a large, curved mouth, her well-shaped head held proudly on the slender neck. Her pale skin betrayed her ancient nordic origins, but it was her hair, which hung almost to her waist, which was her glory. Almost white, it hung thick and straight, gleaming and quivering in the sunlight. Lizzie slumbered on as Leah pushed the iron bar of the skylight to its fullest extent and, on tiptoe, she poked her head through the open window. It was a magical morning, and one, although Leah could not know it then, whose events would shape her whole future.

Netherghyll Hall lay silent. The great house crested the rise like a rose-pink ship, the warm sandstone already refracting the morning sun. Across the fields, like a silver ribbon, lay the Solway Firth, and beyond, the purple

Scottish hills. Drifts of wood pigeons rose from the woods, sheltering the rear of the Hall and filled the morning with their lazy, languid call. It was a small paradise. To the left was the smoke of Whitehaven and to the right lay unseen the town of Workington with its mines and mills. Leah, on tiptoe, stood and gazed happily at the view, then eager to be out in the wonderful morning, she carefully lowered the window, gazing warily at the slumbering Lizzie, fearful lest she wake.

Leah opened the small door of the bedroom and picking up her steel-tipped clogs with one hand and the voluminous folds of her night-gown with the other, she tiptoed down the long flight of back stairs until she came to the deserted kitchen. The banked up embers of the range glowed dully and a fluid cat stretched itself and purred against her bare legs.

'Shh,' Leah whispered warningly as it accompanied her across the flagged floor and over the colourful rag rugs to the back door. She stealthily opened the latch and stepped out, blinking into the bright morning. Swiftly, she pulled on the clogs and set off for the woods. Past the servants privy and the ice house set into the curve of the ground she hurried, the turf buoyant and springy beneath her feet, until she was in the green shelter of the cool summer woods. Soon Leah reached a little tarn. Surrounded by trees, it had been a favourite and secret place of her youth where she and her school friends had splashed and played. Now at sixteen, her freedom had vanished. She and her friends were working hard for a pittance which kept them and their families away from the dreaded workhouse and ever beckoning poverty. Quickly she drew off her night-gown, and with a shudder of pleasurable anticipation, lifted her slim pale arms in a salute to the morning before she slid her body into the cool, clear water.

Hidden in the branches of the oak tree, the boy's eyes widened in shock. For one brief moment he thought he was dreaming and rubbed his eyes in disbelief, thinking some water sprite had mysteriously appeared. He then recognised the little kitchen maid, easily identified by the pale white hair which he had only ever seen peeping from under her cotton cap and which was now floating on the water like a cloak. He had come early that morning to draw the elusive Kingfisher which lived in the sandy banks of the pool. He'd come early because his passion for drawing, or his 'foolishness' as his Mother called it, had to be indulged secretly or invite scorn which he was as yet too sensitive to bear. His one moment of freedom, he thought bitterly, before the day's bustle began, when he would then be at the mercy of his Mother's whims and fancies. Silently recovering himself, he slid his sketchbook on to his knee and began to draw, his hands trembling at first and then swift and sure, committing every turn and twist of the girl's naked body to the pages in his eagerness to capture her youth and beauty. Fed by a spring, the water was crystal clear and her body lay open to his astonished gaze. He felt he had never seen anything so beautiful in his whole life and the sight was to remain in his memory for ever.

When at last Leah stepped out into the shallows, the boy gazed at her wonderingly. He had never seen a naked body before, except those of statues in his art journals. Leah was like some mythical creature, her pale face flushed, her exertions emphasising her glowing skin. The watcher's eyes lingered on her smooth white body, at the small pink tipped breasts and the pale triangle between her long slim legs. Nothing in his brief life had prepared him for the sight. She seemed so natural and innocent and part of her surroundings and he gazed at her in awe. Now she stood close to him, pulling her night-gown over her damp body, bending to put on her clogs and he was overtaken with a rush of feeling which he did not recognise, an ecstasy of feeling so strong that his body shook. The experience left him dizzy and spent and he closed his eyes. When he opened them, the girl had gone.

Hannah

'Eh, Leah! Where've you bin?' asked Lizzie in her soft Northern voice, handing Leah her voluminous petticoats and helping her to do up the buttons of the long serviceable cotton dress and to tie up the ends of her coarse apron or 'brat' as it was called.

'That would be telling, Lizzie,' Leah answered mischievously, hastily stuffing her hair into the white cotton mob cap, knowing only too well that if she told her curious friend she would be surely accompanied for her early morning swim and she valued those moments of privacy before the unending bustle of her day.

'Eh, you are a dark horse, Leah,' Lizzie giggled jealously, 'mebbe you were off to meet a nice young man?'

They both giggled as they scampered down the back stairs to the kitchen. The girls took it in turns to black lead the kitchen range, its fire now resurrected, and to clean the brass knobs and fender. Mrs Hodgson the cook was already at work, her strong brawny arms floury to the elbow, making the daily bread and teacakes that her mistress loved.

'Leah lass,' she grunted, 'after prayers you'll ev to go to the village for some more yeast for me. Ah've run out.'

Her tone was gruff but her small blue eyes shone kindly at Leah for she knew how much Leah missed her Mother and that Leah would run all the way to the village to gain a few minutes with her.

'Yes Mrs Hodgson,' Leah smiled obediently, her eyes thanking the redoubtable woman. After the black leading, she and Lizzie cleaned out the fires and relaid and lit them in the first floor rooms, the drawing room, the dining room and the breakfast room, for although it was summer the prevailing sea winds made the huge rooms, with their floor to ceiling windows, chilly, and Mrs Forbes Robertson fussed over Master James, the son of the house. James was her one and only son and she was always worrying over his delicate disposition.

James, at that moment, crossed the Hall hurriedly, hugging his sketchbook to him, aware that his Mother would put a stop to his early morning expeditions if she knew of them, terrified that his sketchbook would be opened and the explicit pictures of Leah be revealed. As he passed the breakfast room, he noticed the two kitchen maids were now busily laying the table for breakfast. Recognising Leah, his cheeks flushed and he ran up the curving mahogany stairway to the safety of his bedroom. Once inside he threw himself down on the bed and opened his sketchbook. He looked critically at the pages containing the drawings of the naked girl. The magazines and Art Journals carefully chosen by his Mother, humouring his interest, (though at the same time despising it), contained many studies of classical nudes and he knew that his sketches compared favourably with them. His uncle, recognising that James at seventeen should now be aware of certain things, had, in the absence of his Father, taken it upon himself to have a 'man to man talk' with James. In his bluff and kindly way, he had tried to tell James about 'good women' and 'bad' and James knew that one married the 'good' women but enjoyed the 'bad' women. Away at school, populated by adolescent boys, there were interminable discussions about 'the fairer sex' and many huddled viewings of postcards smuggled into cold dormitories. 'One day,' his Uncle had intimated with a cosy wink, he would 'know all about it,' but until then, James was as innocent as the girl in the sketches and he viewed her with a sort of boyish reverence for the beauty of her body and the unexpected reaction it had raised in him. He had captured the independence of the girl in his deft strokes, and the dreamy innocence of her enjoyment sprang from the pages.

The sound of the breakfast gong roused him from his reverie and he hurriedly thrust the sketchbook into his shirt drawer. Any lateness would mean an interrogation from his Mother as to its cause and today he was to go to Workington with his uncle to the Bessemer steel mills to inspect their assets. Making his way downstairs, he joined the household for prayers in the dining room, slipping in hurriedly to stand beside his Mother and his sister. Mrs Forbes Robertson stood imperiously behind the stand, holding the family Bible. She was a floridly handsome woman, her dark hair gleaming and her bright brown eyes snapping behind the steel-rimmed spectacles. She was an unexpected contrast to her pale and slender son. Even James's hair of dark auburn seemed to pale beside her exuberant locks and his hazel eyes appeared a wan reflection of her dark ones. Mrs Forbes Robertson guarded her position in life jealously. Her husband, the Captain, was away so much that she ruled her little kingdom autocratically and with severity. Beside Mrs Forbes Robertson stood Flora, her daughter, a younger handsome copy of her Mother and equally as demanding. The household filed in dutifully, the cook, Leah and Lizzie, Mason the houseman, Mrs Mudd, Mrs Forbes Robertson's maid, only the estate workers who had long been about their work, were not expected to be present. Mrs Forbes Robertson, her blunt fingers holding down the vellum pages of the Bible wherein was contained a list of all the Forbes Robertson forebears, began in her quick impatient voice to admonish them with the scriptures. James glanced furtively at Leah. A strand of still damp hair had escaped from under her white cap and there was a sparkle of excitement in her grey eyes. His glance was caught by Flora, who seeing his interest in Leah looked at him questioningly so that James flushed and turned his head, supposedly listening but not hearing his Mother's hectoring tones.

Leah and Lizzie took turns to wait at the table or help the cook in the kitchen before the daily ritual of cleaning the bedrooms and the stairs. It was Lizzie's turn to wait at table so Leah was free after the seemingly never-ending prayers to retreat to the kitchen. All Mrs Hodgson wanted was yeast, as all the provisions were delivered weekly. Leah's heart beat a little faster as she sped down the back path from the Hall. Only the gentry were allowed to use the imposing broad avenue flanked by oak trees which wound its way to the massive main door of the Hall. Its entrance was guarded by huge wrought iron gates, supported by sandstone pillars on which were carved the coat of arms of the Forbes Robertsons. None of this concerned Leah however, as she ran through the path leading to the back entrance of the Estate. She passed the saddlers' cottage on her left, to her right was the Blacksmiths forge and cottage, and then the cobblers and an assortment of barns and stables and finally at the end of the lane the cottage where the Forester lived. The woods, an important source of income, as well as providing warmth for the Hall, stretched behind the cottages. There were no fancy iron gates here, only a serviceable wooden one hung on the sandstone lintels, and Leah sped through it on to the road which looped round the walled perimeter of the Hall grounds to join up to the main gates. The Hall and its estate was a small claustrophobic self-sufficient world and she was glad to escape from its confines. Leah's heart was beating faster at the thought of seeing her Mother. Leah loved her

Mother with all her heart and soul and her yearly wage of
£7 was given to her to help keep her safe from the ever
threatening workhouse. Leah stopped at the cross roads
which led down to the village, to catch her breath. Opposite
her, the road ran on to a hamlet and a straggle of miners'
cottages. Leah ran on down the hill towards the village. A
mile further on, Leah halted at a small lodge. Geraniums
bloomed at the open windows and checked curtains blew in
the soft breeze. Despite the heat, a trickle of smoke hung
from the chimney, for the fire was the only source of heat
and hot water. Pushing open the gate, Leah went through a
small well-kept garden into a cobbled backyard. A gust of
steam came from the wash house at the corner of the yard.

'Mother,' called Leah anxiously. 'Mother!'

'Leah!' Her Mother came out of the wash house and
Leah flung herself into her arms.

'Oh Mother!' Hannah Fletcher, Leah's Mother, was as
tall as Leah and as slender. Her blonde hair was streaked
with white and the soft skinned face was lined, but the
mouth was still firm and the gaze was uncompromising.
Life had not treated her kindly. An intelligent girl, she had
worked hard at school to become a pupil teacher and had
married 'the young school master.' Alas, the 'young school
master' had died of the ever-present scourge of
tuberculosis, leaving his young bride with a small annuity
from her dead parents and Leah to bring up single handed.
Only the pittance she made teaching at the village school,
which was dependent on the success of the stringent and
dreaded inspections, and Leah's money, kept her from dire
poverty, but she considered herself lucky because she was
educated and had been able to educate her only daughter,
teaching her to read and write.

'Leah,' the grey eyes were tender as she held her
daughter at arm's length.

'I'm on the way to the village for yeast for Mrs Hodgson!' Leah gasped, 'but I've run all the way and if I run all the way back, I'll have time for a cup of tea. Is there any cake?' she asked childishly.

'Yes, Leah,' her Mother laughed. 'Slow down! I'll put the kettle on for your return.'

She laughed as Leah detached herself and ran off, but her eyes were misty as she put on the kettle and went to the scullery to get the much desired cake. Families in those days were most harshly split and only saw each other for brief intervals. Girls in service were usually only given one day off every six months to visit their families.

'Thank you Mrs Hodgson,' she murmured under her breath to the kind cook, who, as often as she could, created opportunities for Leah and Lizzie to visit their families. Leah ran on, over the main road and up the hill to the village. Ghyllside was a typical mining village, a huddle of grimy terraced houses dominated by a pub, The Punch Bowl, and a large forbidding church and a small village school, with a school house attached. High walls surrounded the school and its segregated playground. No childish voices echoed from its walls as most of the children were on 'holiday' helping the farmers in the fields to gain precious pennies for their families. Leah passed the village privy, and smiled on hearing muffled voices. The village communal privy had three seats each for men and women, divided by a substantial wall. All three doors on the women's side were closed and Leah stifled a muffled giggle imagining the occupants having a good chat. It was the village gossiping place and often a source of a moment's peace for the hard-working miners' wives, living lives in shifts. Leah passed the Miners' Welfare and finally stood in front of Becks', the Grocers. Leah pushed open the door, the brass bell jangled importantly and she stepped into the cool dark interior. Mounds of lard and butter stood on marble slabs on the counter, rusty coloured hams hung from hooks on the beams. Behind the counter, banks of glass labelled drawers rose to the wooden ceiling. Mr Beck came smoothly out from the gloom at the back of the shop. His immaculate white shirt gleamed, his sleeves pushed up and held by expanding wire arm bands lest they should get sullied by his produce. His white apron was creaseless, his brilliantined hair, parted meticulously down the middle, glistened as if it had been polished and he stood ramrod straight like the soldier he had once been. Even the jars and huge painted canisters of tea, sugar and flour seemed to stand to attention in his presence.

'What an unexpected pleasure, Miss Leah,' he said in his deep voice.

'What can I get for you this lovely morning?'

'Only a half pound of yeast please, Mr Beck,' Leah requested, 'and how are you?'

'As well as can be expected, thank you Leah,' Mr Beck replied, bringing forward a block of yeast, 'the warm weather is good for old war wounds.'

Mr Beck had fought for Queen and country in the Boer War.

'And how is your dear Mother?' he enquired, as he cut off the crumbly yeast on a marble slab and weighed it on large brass scales, sighing with satisfaction at the accuracy of his cutting.

'She appears well, thank you Mr Beck,' answered Leah politely, for it was no secret in the village that the handsome shopkeeper harboured cherished thoughts of her Mother.

'In fact,' she said impatiently as Mr Beck tore off a strip of brown paper and expertly made a cone in which to put the yeast, 'I've run all the way so that I might have a moment with her.' Deftly tucking the flap into the cornet of paper, Mr Beck took the proffered pence quickly.

'Er… are you too old for chocolate, Leah?' he enquired.

'Oh no, Mr Beck,' Leah replied delightedly as she took the bar of dark York chocolate.

'Thank you very much. You're very kind.'

'And, er, here is one for your dear Mother with, er, my compliments.' Mr Beck held out a second bar to Leah, a slight flush rising beneath his clean shaven cheeks.

'Well…' said Leah dubiously, not knowing what her Mother would feel about an unsolicited gift, then anxious to be off, she took the proffered bar, thanked him again, and set off once more. Leah stood impatiently at the side of the main road to let a rather grand car pass on its way to Workington. Had she looked more closely she would have seen the 'young Master' and his uncle sitting in the well-padded interior, but Leah's mind was full of thoughts of her Mother. At last, the lodge was in sight. She ran down the path breathlessly.

'I'm back, Mother,' she called breathlessly.

'I'm here.' Hannah Fletcher came out of the back door immediately.

'Slowly. Slowly, child,' she admonished, holding out her welcoming arms to Leah. Arms entwined, they went into the kitchen. The lodge had only two rooms, a living room/kitchen and a bedroom but it was as neat and pretty as a new pin. The kitchen was large enough to hold a table and two chairs, and an old horsehair chaise lounge upholstered in black pinoleum. There was a sideboard with a mahogany mirror above it and two large mahogany bookcases with books spilling out of them, for reading was a passion with Hannah and she took the long bus ride once a week into Whitehaven to change her books at the Public Library so generously funded by Andrew Carnegie. A rather fine mirror hung above the mantelpiece and two well-executed oil paintings hung on the whitewashed walls. The black range with its stone sink beside it gave an indication of a poor but genteel background. Hannah, the youngest daughter of an impoverished clergyman, had made a love marriage with the even poorer schoolmaster and only the few delicate ornaments from her family home revealed her intellectual background, but Hannah did not complain. Compared to some, such as the miners families, she was well off. Although poor, she was warm and dry and she had Leah who loved her and filled her heart with joy.

Seated opposite each other over a cup of tea and the longed for cake, the pair smiled with pleasure at each other.

'Oh Mother, I do miss you!' Leah cried, licking the last crumbs off her fingers in a childlike gesture.

'I miss you too, Leah,' her Mother agreed seriously, 'but how lucky we are that you found service so near to me and we are not separated as some poor families are who see each other but once a year. Even if,' she added with a smile, 'you do have to work for Dragon Lady!' This was the nickname, entirely deserved, that Leah had bestowed on the formidable Mrs Forbes Robertson.

'I know,' replied Leah, equally as serious, 'but don't you ever think, Mother, how unfair things are? You are as well educated, if not better educated than she. Don't you think that life is unfair and unequal? Why should she live in a big house and have lots of money when you have not? Oh, not that I do not love my home,' she added hastily, seeing Hannah's grave look. She reached over the table to take Hannah's hand.

'One day, Mother,' she said confidently, 'things will change, you will see. In the meantime,' she added mischievously, 'Mr Beck has sent you a bar of chocolate.'

'Oh Leah,' Hannah reproved, a flush rising to her pale cheeks, 'You should not have accepted it.'

'It's all right, Mother,' laughed Leah, 'I have one, too,' and she brandished a rather melted bar of chocolate.

'I must go,' she added hastily, glancing at the clock on the wall, 'I shall see you as soon as ever I can, Mother.' She gave her Mother a warm embrace. Her Mother stood and watched her as she ran up the road until a bend obscured her view. Straightening her back, she went back into the cottage and sat down heavily at the table. She heard Leah's voice echoing in her head, 'One day, Mother, things will change.' She sighed. Youth was always optimistic but who could change the scheme of things? Picking up the plates and cups, she went over to the sink and started to wash them.

*

Nothing in James' wildest nightmares had prepared him for the sight and sound of the great steel mill. Aghast, he stood by his uncle, clasping his linen handkerchief to his nose as they toured the mill. Speech was impossible and his uncle communicated by sign language with the dirty and sweaty foremen. Men as depersonalised as ants, laboured with the molten metal in the pounding clanging fiery inferno. They hauled huge ladles to pour the molten metal into thick moulds. Thick steel ingots were being rolled to extend them. The heat, the noise and the smell of human sweat was almost more than James could bear. He put his hand over his mouth lest the rising bile would betray his sensitivity and disgust. When at last they went outside, James gulped the tainted air in great breaths.

'Well, lad,' his uncle said complacently, 'we won't lose our money with that lot. Especially if there's a war coming. We'll be bloody millionaires.' James had never heard his uncle swear before and it seemed to add a strange gravity to the pronouncement.

'A war, uncle?' he asked wonderingly.

'Aye lad, a war,' his uncle replied grimly. 'It's just over the horizon. It won't take much to light the fire until we're all in the flames.' Seeing his nephew's alarmed expression, he clapped him on the shoulder reassuringly.

'Don't worry, lad. I'm too old for it and you're too young. We'll just be bloody millionaires.'

*

There was an air of subdued excitement in the cavernous kitchen when Leah returned.

'Hurry up, lass,' grumbled the cook cheerfully as Leah put the yeast on the scrubbed pine table, 'The mistress wants us in the dining room.'

'What for?' Leah asked curiously, for it was a rare occurrence for Mrs Forbes Robertson to interrupt the daily routine of scrubbing and polishing.

'Ah doan't know, Leah,' replied the cook, 'You're as wise as ah am.'

Mrs Forbes Robertson stood ramrod straight and surveyed her little army with asperity. Flora stood beside her with a smirk of satisfaction on her face.

'I have heard from the Captain today,' said Mrs Forbes Robertson without preamble.

'He is to return Monday week. He is,' she paused for effect, 'bringing an American visitor with him.'

An American! She could have caused no more amazement if she had announced the man in the moon was visiting. Her eyes gleamed with satisfaction.

'An American,' she repeated.

Arrival

The Hall was in a fever of excitement. The silver was polished until you could see your face in it. The brass and copper shone, crystal was washed and rinsed with vinegar, and polished, carpets were hauled outside and beaten with the big bamboo beaters, curtains brushed, windows cleaned, bedding aired, clothes pressed and goffered, stairs waxed with sweet smelling lavender-scented polish, the brass stair-rods polished till they shone, no greater effort could have been made if royalty itself were visiting. Everything was ready for the Captain and his visitor. The entire household of the Hall were in a fever of impatience to see 'the American' and all guarded some fantasy about him. Mrs Forbes Robertson hoped that he would be rich and famous and impress the neighbours. Flora dreamed of a handsome prince who would sweep her off her feet and take her to the new world. James hoped for a born raconteur who would talk about the Wild West and Red Indians. Mrs Hodgson hoped that he would like her roast pheasant and old English syllabub, and even Mrs Mudd, Mrs Forbes Robertson's maid, yearned for a stranger who would see that she was really a princess in disguise. Everyone had their own particular fantasy. Everyone, that is, except the little maids who worked from dawn to dusk and were so worn out with their cleaning that they fell into a dreamless sleep as soon as their heads touched the lumpy pillows in their creaking iron bedstead.

The little port of Whitehaven was thriving. The Cumberland of 1909 was a county rich with mines and iron. The export of coal and iron kept the Solway ports busy. Each little town had its own shipping industry. It was rumoured that at Maryport, where they launched their ships broadside into the River Ellen, that a man could walk from ship to ship right across the great docks. Captain Forbes Robertson stood on the Queen's jetty looking about him with satisfaction. All was hustle and bustle and obvious prosperity.

'It'll be good to sleep on dry land tonight, O'Neill,' Captain Forbes Robertson remarked happily to his visitor who was surveying the bustling scene on the Queen's wharf with evident enjoyment.

'Yes,' the man beside him agreed readily, 'it will be good to breathe fresh air tonight instead of the ozone.'

The American was tall and slim with an extremely handsome face and a shock of blonde hair, the expensive cut of his clothes marked him out as a stranger. His colouring and his name, Taylor O'Neill, gave proof of his not too distant Irish ancestry. He gazed about him curiously and his vivid blue eyes shone with interest. The Captain interrupted his thoughts. He turned to the man at his side.

'Come on, O'Neill,' he said authoritatively, 'yonder is my pony and trap waiting for us. I thought you would enjoy that mode of transport rather than using one of those new fangled motor cars. We will see more of the countryside.' Taylor O'Neill chuckled appreciatively.

'Excellent,' he replied cordially, his clipped Bostonian accent a marked contrast to the Captain's slow Northern speech. The Captain led Taylor to where a pony and a shining trap stood waiting. The driver doffed his hat respectfully and the two men climbed inside, the American a good foot taller than his companion and having difficulty settling his long lanky legs into the confined space. After a short delay as the Captain asked of news of home from the driver, they set off on the slow journey to the Hall, the Captain replying jocularly to the many shouted greetings and patiently answering his guest's questions. The road wound its way up the long hill out of Whitehaven and along the coast. All along the coast stood evidence of coal mining, huge pit wheels and colliery buildings surrounded by slag banks making a crude and schizophrenic contrast to the rolling green fields and the glimpse of the Lakeland hills miles away to the right. They looked like an artist's vision of hell in the beautiful day and it was hard to imagine that far below, men toiled half-naked, like beasts, to mine the 'black diamonds' and to make the rich landowners richer. Taylor was amazed to see how close and clear Scotland looked just a few miles over the Solway. When he mentioned this, the Captain gave a snort.

'Fought them for years,' he said disparagingly, 'and they still hate us and us them. The only good thing which came out of Scotland,' he ruminated, 'was whisky... although there are some damn fine engineers,' he added grudgingly. The trap proceeded at a leisurely pace, now and then slowing to a halt as the Captain exchanged news and greetings with passing acquaintances in traps, like themselves. Taylor and the Captain swapped desultory conversation but Taylor was so involved with looking at the scenery that most of the journey was made in silence. Taylor was intrigued by this small microcosm of England. Second generation Irish from Boston, he was proud of the 'New World' and its constitution which proclaimed that 'all men are born equal'. The dynamism and free thinking of his country excited him and inspired him. He caught echoes of his own thoughts in the tide of rising Socialism sweeping Europe and believed passionately that everyone should have a chance to prove themselves. The Industrial Revolution had galvanised Britain to be a thriving and dynamic nation but its overt feudalism appalled him and he was shocked by the contradiction between great wealth and great poverty which was so apparent in the cities he visited. He sighed as the trap bowled in between the great sandstone lintels but then cheered up at the thought of a warm bath, good food and a soft bed, all of which he would shortly enjoy. He had met the Captain in Liverpool where they were doing business with the same ship broker and the unlikely friendship had begun, sparked by the curiosity they had in each other and their shared work ethic. Although there was more than twenty years difference between them, they liked and respected each other. Taylor had been pleased to receive an invitation to the Captain's home and intrigued by the tales of the American 'pirate' John Paul Jones, born in Scotland who had attempted to fire the ships in Whitehaven harbour, a century before. Far from home, he looked forward to some home comfort and, albeit briefly, family life.

No one at the Hall was disappointed by the 'American'. His easy charm, friendly manner and innate kindness endeared him to all and made him an instant favourite. Even Mrs Forbes Robertson bloomed under his attention and changed her stiff bombazines for soft silk and taffetas. The Hall was in a fever. There were comings and goings with the neighbours, parties for tennis, parties for shooting, picnic parties, luncheons and dinners, all with the express intention of showing off the prize of Netherghyll Hall, Taylor O'Neill, who was indubitably a success. Throughout it all he watched, learned and listened to a way of life which was surely and inexorably doomed.

'You know,' he said seriously to the Captain one morning as they breakfasted alone, Mrs Forbes Robertson and Flora too tired to rise after the previous night's exertions, 'you know Henry, you remind me of a medieval feudal baron.' The Captain listened attentively, stifling a hasty reply, as he had come to respect the intelligence and perception of his visitor. 'All these people, a pyramid of servants with you at the apex existing only to serve you and your family.' Leah was leaning with her back surreptitiously against the sideboard for she and the other servants, although up late, did not have the luxury of being able to rest in bed. She jerked upright, dumbfounded to hear anyone talk in such a way to the Captain.

'I see no wrong in that,' replied the Captain tersely, his face reddening. 'I provide my servants with needful and gainful employment. Without me they would have no work save in the mines or mills or at other menial tasks. And without work,' he said warningly, 'there is only the workhouse.'

'Not so,' contradicted Taylor, 'for in my country each person has the freedom to be what he aspires to be, all men are equal. Why,' he added, 'my own family two generations ago were Irish peasants, driven by famine to the New World. They were not trapped in a servile system.'

The Captain flushed.

'Here it is different. People know where they belong, and let me remind you that a lot of your country's wealth is founded on slavery.'

'Are you then saying,' said Taylor heatedly, 'that slavery is a good thing and that a country cannot generate wealth without some form of slavery? And,' he added slyly, 'I do believe that Whitehaven sheltered slave ships in the not too distant past?'

'Aye, true enough,' the Captain agreed shortly, 'but all that is many years ago. Now we have stability.'

'No doubt the Russian Czar thinks so too whilst all talk about Revolution,' countered Taylor swiftly. 'I tell you there is a tide of Socialism sweeping through Europe which will wash all the old structures away for ever.'

Leah listened intently, Taylor's utterings mirrored her half-formed thoughts and her longings for better things for herself and her Mother. She was disappointed when the conversation turned to events in Europe but her interest was caught when she heard Taylor ask, 'Was it not Jean Jacques Rousseau who said "All men are born free but everywhere in chains"?'

'You are not then saying that my servants are in chains!' ejaculated the Captain, becoming vastly irritated by Taylor's comments. 'To what shall I free them, for what?'

'Free them by educating them,' came the prompt reply. 'Make them free in thought and then they can stand beside you as friends and not as servants. Why,' he added dangerously, swinging round and regarding Leah, 'do you need someone to wait on us at table whilst we eat?' Leah returned his fiery gaze steadily and did not lower her eyes. Taylor was caught by the level grey stare until the Captain, swinging round also, glared at Leah as if he had seen a strange and rare insect. Leah lowered her eyes quickly but not before the infuriated Captain had seen in them a gleam of defiance. He struck the table.

'By God, you go too far O'Neill. You are a guest in my house.'

'Of course,' interjected Taylor quickly, 'I do apologise Henry. I go too far and presume upon our friendship.' He held out his hand winningly.

'Please forgive my New World ways.'

Slightly mollified, the Captain shook Taylor's hand.

'Accepted O'Neill,' he said, waving his hand to Leah dismissively. 'You may go.'

'Do you know her name?' she heard Taylor ask, but could not hear the reply as she closed the door quietly behind her. The conversation had excited Leah and with the bar of chocolate from Mr Beck, she bribed Lizzie to change duties with her the next week in the hope of hearing more. However, there was no more conversation to feed her ideas during the next few days although each morning she was rewarded with a warm smile from Taylor which she returned unashamedly. Leah stood each morning ramrod straight, fearful to move lest she disturb the conversations which flowed freely when 'the ladies' were not present. Their wide ranging talk interested her and she resolved to take more interest in the events of the outside world. One morning near the end of Taylor's visit, the talk turned to war. The Captain agreed gloomily that the signs were bad, however he perked up visibly remarking that the order books at the steel mills were full and that there was virtually full employment for all.

'Henry,' said Taylor prophetically, 'if, when war comes, your fully employed men will be taken for cannon fodder and your women left to weep. The old order,' he looked across at Leah, for he had taken to positioning himself where he could watch her, 'will be swept away.' Leah did not bow her head at his swift glance. She looked openly without embarrassment into the American's blue eyes, hers widening in understanding. Leah was to remember that conversation vividly in years to come.

*

Disaster struck one rainy afternoon, two days before the end of Taylor's visit. The Captain was busy about his estates because he too had to return to sea in the near future. Taylor, Mrs Forbes Robertson, Flora and James were sitting in the morning room. Rain streamed down the window panes and the conversation turned to Taylor's travels in Europe. James had turned the conversation to Florence and was eagerly asking Taylor about the artistic treasures he had seen, his enthusiasm kindled by the subject close to his heart. He was uncharacteristically animated much to Mrs Forbes Robertson's delight.

'James too is an artist,' she grandly informed Taylor. James flushed to the roots of his hair.

'Mother,' he said in abject embarrassment, 'you cannot call me an artist in the same breath as Raphael or Michael Angelo.'

'Nonsense James,' Mrs Forbes Robertson bristled, 'go and get your sketchbook to show Mr O'Neill so that he may make comment on your efforts.'

James stiffened in horror. The sketches of Leah were still in his book and he often looked at them, not in a prurient way but to reassure himself that he had captured the essence of innocence portrayed.

'No Mother,' he gasped, 'Mr O'Neill will not wish to see the doodlings of an amateur.'

'I should be pleased to see them,' said Taylor kindly, for he had been amazed at the difference in James's demeanour whilst he had been talking about the subject he loved. Up until then he had thought him a dull boy with not much to say.

'I'll get the book,' interrupted Flora mischievously, piqued that James had been the centre of attention and not she.

'You don't know where it is,' pleaded James desperately, springing up to restrain her.

'James. Sit down,' his Mother commanded, her tone brooking no opposition.

'I'll find it,' smirked Flora triumphantly, eager to exacerbate her brother's discomfort and make herself the focus of attention. James sank back in his chair, as if turned to stone, terrified of the imminent discovery. Taylor looked at him keenly, puzzled at the reaction, surely he thought the sketches could not be so bad? After what seemed like hours to James, Flora entered the room waving the sketchbook above her head.

'Give it to me!' James shouted pleadingly, stretching a trembling hand to snatch it from her.

'James!' his Mother's tone was savage.

'James. Manners. Give it to me!' she demanded coldly to Flora.

'Wait,' called James, 'there are some pages I do not wish you to see.'

He attempted to pull the sketchbook from Flora and it fell from her grasp on to the carpet. The pages fluttered as they fell.

Leah was in the kitchen when she was summoned to the morning room by Lizzie who had answered the frantic summons of the bell.

'What do they want me for?' asked Leah as they walked along the passage.

'Mebbe they want to know where you go some mornings,' said Lizzie sourly, 'and about that young man you meet.' she hazarded, her fat face full of spite. Leah looked at her in amazement, taken aback by the venom in her voice. Leah entered the room awkwardly, astonished by the scene which met her eyes. Mrs Forbes Robertson stood by the fireplace, her face white with rage, holding a sketchbook rigidly in her hand. James was sobbing uncontrollably in the arms of the American who was gently trying to calm him. Flora, her face pale also, had a malicious twist of her mouth reflecting her satisfaction at her brother's discomfort. Leah stood still waiting. Mrs Forbes Robertson thrust the sketchbook towards Leah with a shaking hand.

'Deny these are pictures of you!' Mrs Forbes Robertson's voice was shaking and high-pitched. Leah took the sketchbook and looked disbelievingly at the sketches. She began to shake uncontrollably.

'But Mam,' she said, 'I know nothing of these.'

'Deny it is you!' Mrs Forbes Robertson screamed furiously.

'I cannot deny it, Mam,' Leah's voice trembled.

'I have been swimming in the tarn during the hot weather but,' a crimson flush stained her cheeks, 'I never knew,' she turned to James pitifully, 'that someone was… watching me.'

'I'm sorry. I'm sorry!' gasped James, 'you were so beautiful.'

'Beautiful!' Mrs Forbes Robertson seemed to erupt with rage.

'Beautiful? A hussy who swims naked for every man to view?'

'It was not like that!' interrupted Leah, 'it was so hot, and it is a secret place.'

'So secret that my son could see you and sketch you naked!' retaliated Mrs Forbes Robertson vindictively. 'You are dismissed, girl. Instantly. Get your bag and leave this minute. I will not have you stay another minute. I will make it my business to see that you are never employed anywhere near here ever again!'

'But Mam,' cried Leah, frightened, 'I have nowhere to go. My Mother is a widow and needs my money…' her voice shook uncontrollably.

'You should have thought of that before you shamed her!' came the swift reply. At the thought of the shame this would bring to her Mother, tears poured down Leah's pale cheeks.

'Oh please Mam, please don't do this!' she begged.

Taylor intervened.

'The girl has done no harm, madam,' he said to Mrs Forbes Robertson, 'please reconsider.'

'No harm!' she looked at him with scorn. 'She has corrupted my son.'

She turned to James, 'Get to your room James. You will be sent away as soon as possible. Remain there till your Father returns. And you,' she swung round to Leah, and raising her hand as if to strike her, she pulled herself back, 'and *you,* leave this house for ever.'

Leaving

The Captain returned to find Netherghyll Hall in an uproar. His wife was in hysterics and his American friend packing his bags ready to leave a day earlier than expected. His son had barricaded himself into his bedroom and his daughter was waiting with a queer little smirk of satisfaction to tell him a garbled story of James and a naked maid. Eventually, when he had listened to his daughter and calmed his wife, he heard the whole story. Being a 'man of the world', he laughed and dismissed the tale with a contemptuous shrug.

'Your son,' he said to his wife, 'is an artistic milksop. It will have done him no harm to have seen a naked girl, especially a maid. Far better to have these sorts of experiences at an early age, my dear,' he said smugly, 'and better at home than in a bawdy house. Now then my dear,' he put a kindly arm around his wife's shoulders, 'the running of the house is up to you. It is in an uproar. It is up to you as mistress of this house to show the servants how little we regard this incident and how little disturbed we are. I trust the girl has gone?' he added as an afterthought.

'Yes, Henry,' his wife answered dutifully, secretly pleased that her husband had acted in so masterful a way.

'I dismissed her immediately.'

'Good,' the Captain applauded, 'we do not wish to put too much temptation in the boy's way do we? Remember my dear, that sons of wealthy families have a process of selection to go through, eh?' He winked at his wife in a knowing way, who tossed her head and pretended to be scandalised. The Captain knocked on James's door and said in a tone which brooked no opposition, 'James. Open this door at once, sir.' James, dreading the moment of shame when he saw his Father, opened the door slowly. His Father walked into the room and James was amazed to hear his Father say, 'Well James, you have discovered the fair sex at last.' He was even more amazed to hear his Father continue, 'Sooner or later, James, all men must have their experience, or how would they know what to do on their wedding night?' The Captain laughed a great rollicking laugh and clapped him on the shoulder.

'Sir,' James stammered, 'It was not like that. The girl thought she was on her own and I hid so that I might draw her. She was so... beautiful,' he continued wistfully.

'Aye James,' said his Father bluffly, 'You will see many more beauties in your time, I warrant. That's the way of the world. However,' he added warningly, 'take my advice. Never get mixed up with the servants. It is too near home. Should you wish for any particular female company,' he winked again, 'I will fix it for you or if I am away from home your uncle will see you are not, er, disappointed.'

'But the girl has lost her position,' James said dubiously, only too pleased at his Father's reaction, especially as he had feared a beating.

'She is young James,' his Father intoned sententiously, 'there are plenty of positions for young, and,' he paused, 'pretty maids.' Indeed he found it difficult to visualise which maid Leah was he had so little regard for his 'inferiors' as he considered them. He was far more comfortable when he was at sea and not dealing with these tiresome matters.

'You see Taylor,' he remarked to his guest over breakfast, before Taylor's departure, 'men must sow their wild oats and if not with these sort of girls then with whom?' He speared a sausage with great vigour.

'I must disagree with you Henry,' Taylor said quietly, 'and I fear I have spent much of my stay disagreeing with you. What of the girl? Does she command no respect?' He thought of Leah's grey eyes and in a brief flash the picture of her he had seen in the sketchbook flashed disturbingly into his mind.

'The girl now has no job and no character. She was not to blame for what happened. Your son hid to draw her in her innocent nakedness. She was given no chance to defend herself against accusations about herself.'

'Ah well,' the Captain replied brusquely, 'It would appear the girl is no better than she should or else why was she swimming naked? And after all, boys will be boys and it is all part of growing up. Some boys would have done more than draw…' he leered suggestively at Taylor. 'It is all part of growing up. So the boy sees a naked maid. Is it the end of the world?' Taylor stayed silent. How could he, an American, change the hypocritical snobbishness of the British. Still, he felt sorry for Leah and in some ways responsible for her plight. On an impulse, before his belongings were collected, he knocked on James's bedroom door.

'I have come to bid you farewell James,' he explained, 'for I leave today.' James opened the door and gazed shamefacedly at the American.

'I am ashamed,' he blurted.

'James,' said Taylor gently, 'I have two things to say to you and I hope you will hear me out.'

James nodded silently, for he liked the tall American.

'Firstly,' said Taylor, 'you have the makings of an artist. Nurture your talent, James, for I see that will make you happy.' James nodded again, almost overcome at being treated kindly when he had expected scorn.

'Secondly,' added Taylor, 'a great wrong has been done to that young girl.' James flushed to the roots of his hair.

'I know sir,' he assented, 'I hope that one day I might right that wrong but I am to return to Sedbergh School next week and I fear I shall have no chance to do anything. My Mother will see to that,' he added grimly. Taylor put out his hand.

'Then shake hands upon it James, for I believe you will right it one day if you are able. Now I must take my leave. I bid you a warm farewell, James.'

★

Before he left, Taylor sought out Lizzie.

'I wish you to give your friend this,' he said, handing a small package to the dumbfounded Lizzie. 'Here is a sovereign for your trouble.' He pressed the coin into Lizzie's grubby palm.

'It may be weeks before I see her, sir,' she faltered, her brain racing with the thought that Mr O'Neill as well as the young master had had dealings with Leah. The sly bitch, she thought vindictively, with a face as smooth as butter.

'I shall know from your friend,' said Taylor firmly, guessing in which direction Lizzie's thoughts lay, 'as to whether she receives it.'

'Yes sir,' said Lizzie sullenly, tucking the packet into her apron pocket.

'And not a word to anyone,' added Taylor warningly.

Lizzie brightened at the thought of a conspiracy, and what a good bit of gossip she could tell when the American had gone, she thought. Taylor made his farewells to the household and set off on the long road to Whitehaven, never guessing as he passed the lodge that Leah was so near.

★

Safe in her Mother's protective arms, Leah sobbed out her shame and outrage. Trembling and ashen she had carried her suitcase with her few possessions down the road to Hannah's lodge. Hannah held her daughter close, hushing her as if she were a baby.

'There, there,' she soothed, stroking the pale white hair over and over, 'it's all right, Leah. It's all right.' But she knew that it was not 'all right.' Her rage rose like bile in her throat at the thought of James hidden, spying upon her daughter, but more than that her anger grew at the thought of Leah's summary dismissal.

'What am I to do?' moaned Leah, 'Where am I to go without a character?' Her pale face suddenly looked old and haggard.

'Hush child,' said her Mother automatically, 'we'll find a way. Hush now.' and she held open her arms as Leah cried for her lost innocence. That evening as Leah slept in her Mother's bed, exhausted by her emotions, Hannah Fletcher came to a decision. Skewering her hat firmly on her head with the steel hatpins and shrugging on her threadbare coat, she walked the long road to Netherghyll Hall. It was a beautiful evening. The summer light was paling and the swallows twisted and dived in the pale clear air as she reached the crossroads to the Hall. Hannah was blind to all but her purpose. Her face suddenly hardening and the colour of her eyes deepening to the colour of charcoal, she took the road to the Hall that the gentry used. There was no way now after the wrong done to her daughter that she would creep in through the back gate and knock at the kitchen door like a servant. She lengthened her stride and pushed open the great iron gates, walking purposefully up the drive lined with rhododendrons and azaleas, shaded by oaks in full leaf. Leah's voice echoed in her head. 'Why should they have such things and we live in penury?' Why indeed? she thought, anger fuelling her determination to right the wrong done to her innocent child. Without faltering she walked up to the huge front door and banged on the iron knocker. There was a pause then the door opened slowly. Lizzie looked at Hannah Fletcher in bemusement. Although she had never met Hannah the striking similarity to Leah made her instantly recognisable.

'Yes. Er…' Lizzie enquired, instinctively knowing she need not address this shabby woman as 'Marm' ('As white as a sheet she was,' she confided later to her eager audience downstairs. 'There's been some queer goings on here what with her walking up to the front door as bold as brass.') For like most servants Lizzie was as snobbish as her masters.

'I wish to see your mistress,' said Hannah commandingly, her natural authority asserting itself and her fine bearing giving emphasis to her request.

'Yes. Er.' Lizzie scurried away to get Mrs Forbes Robertson, her natural curiosity at fever patch. Nervously she knocked at the sitting room door and entered at the peremptory. 'Enter.' Mrs Forbes Robertson was playing bezique with Flora.

'Please Miss,' Lizzie stuttered, 'There's a person to see you.'

'Who is it?' demanded Mrs Forbes Robertson testily, 'How many times must I tell you Lizzie to find out who it is before you indicate if I am available.' She got up impatiently and swept into the Hall.

'Well. Who are you?' she demanded imperiously although a quick inspection of Hannah's person and the startling likeness to her daughter gave her an immediate answer.

'I am Leah Fletcher's Mother and I would like to discuss with you the incident which caused you to dismiss her,' said Hannah quietly.

'There is nothing to discuss,' Mrs Forbes Robertson interrupted haughtily. 'I have dismissed the girl and that is all there is to it.'

'You have dismissed her unfairly,' Hannah countered hotly, 'You have dismissed her without a character and that is unfair.'

'Unfair? Unfair?' snarled Mrs Forbes Robertson. 'Who are you to say unfair? Do you deny she was swimming nude for all to see?'

'Leah is only a child,' said Hannah desperately, 'she thought she was safe in her secret place.'

'Safe,' countered Mrs Forbes Robertson. 'To cast off her clothes is not a safe thing to do!'

'But your son spied on her,' countered Hannah, 'and drew her. No doubt he would have shown his,' she paused and then her voice sharpened with scorn, 'no doubt he would have shown all his friends at school. This is not the way of a gentleman.'

'I do not need the likes of you to tell me whether or not my son is a gentleman,' hissed Mrs Forbes Robertson in fury, 'no doubt your girl swam there to attract just such attention.' Ignoring Leah's Mother's cry of protest, she said, 'Now. Leave my house at once.' She turned away dismissively. Hannah stretched out her hand and caught Mrs Forbes Robertson's sleeve.

'At least give my child a reference,' she pleaded. 'Without a reference she will not be able to gain employment.' Mrs Forbes Robertson shrugged off the detaining hand contemptuously.

'Lizzie. Show this person out,' she commanded.

'There is no need.' Hannah drew herself up with dignity and turned on her heel.

'You are no lady,' she said contemptuously over her shoulder to Mrs Forbes Robertson as she walked past the dumbfounded Lizzie. The news was all over Ghyllside in a matter of hours. The men were titillated by the scandal and most respectable matrons thought, The girl was stupid, but all agreed on Hannah Fletcher's courage in going to 'the Big House'. Listening to the gossip in his shop the next morning a small smile of admiration passed over the face of the handsome shopkeeper. Half way through the morning he wiped his hands, turned the 'open' sign to 'closed', put on his jacket and curly brimmed bowler and began the long walk to the lodge.

Whitehaven

'Come away in.'

Rachel Beck was like her brother, as neat and fresh as a new pin. Everything about her shone, her pale skin, her glossy black hair, her worn black boots. Her clothes, although of poor stuff, were clean and pressed. Leah liked her on sight and the warm and Motherly tone she used, although she would possibly be only one or two years older, warmed Leah's heart. The room behind Beck's groceries in Whitehaven was sparse, but a coal fire burned in the small grate and a kettle sang on the hearth. Wilson Beck had written to his sister, warning her of Leah's imminent arrival and although he had not told her of all the reasons for Leah's dismissal, believing correctly that in time Leah would give Rachel her confidence, Rachel knew that Leah had been cruelly treated. Rachel drew Leah towards the fire.

'Leah,' she said excitedly, 'don't take off your coat. I think we might have found you a position.'

Leah's pale face flushed.

'Oh, Rachel,' she cried, 'that would be wonderful. But,' she added doubtfully, 'what about a reference?'

Rachel smiled.

'My brother's reference would suffice,' she said proudly.

'The position is at Miss Hartley's Refreshment Rooms just up the way. We,' she stopped and blushed prettily, 'that is my brother, supplies Miss Hartley with all her provisions.

Miss Hartley likes my brother and would be pleased to do him a favour.' She laughed prettily.

'Truth to tell, Leah,' she smiled confidently, 'I think Miss Hartley looks favourably on him.'

'Oh.' Leah smiled in confusion unable to see the handsome grocer as an object of desire. Her grey eyes filled with unexpected tears and she dashed them away proudly asking at the same time in a shaky voice, 'Why are you so kind to me, Rachel?'

Rachel smiled and then said softly, 'Anyone with eyes in their heads, Leah, only has to look in your face and see the honesty shining through. Now,' she changed the subject quickly, 'let us away. Miss Hartley knows we are coming.'

The girls walked through the shop.

'I shan't be long Brian,' Rachel informed the attentive young man behind the counter.

'Brian and I are going to be married,' she vouchsafed shyly to Leah, 'once we have saved up some money.'

The two girls walked up Tangier Street. Leah looked about her with interest. She was used to the relative quiet of the Hall and was taken aback by the hustle and bustle. They paused at the four-storey warehouse of Metcalf's Wholesale Groceries and avoided workmen rolling a 'hogshead' of tobacco into Messrs George Jackson's Tobacco, an import and export business further up the street. The girls dallied awhile, watching in amusement at the sight of a goose helping his master with a sandwich board promotion for Maypole Tea. On the corner of Tangier and Duke Street was a fine building of Italianate style which Rachel told Leah was yet another Grocery and Tea warehouse. The grandiose co-operative building loomed on the other corner. Leah would have liked to stop and stare at these buildings but Rachel urged her on until they came to Miss Hartley's Refreshment Rooms. The shop was only three minutes away from the busy railway station, its double-fronted windows temptingly displaying cakes and confectioneries. Miss Hartley was a tall, sweet-faced lady of perhaps thirty years.

She gave Leah a penetrating stare from a pair of disconcertingly sharp blue eyes.

'Let me see your hands, Leah,' she asked in a voice so quiet Leah strained to hear it. Leah stretched out her small well-shaped hands already marked by work.

'Turn them over,' Miss Hartley requested.

Leah did so in silence.

'Excellent,' Miss Hartley murmured. Her bright blue gaze surveyed Leah from head to toe.

'Excellent. Well, Leah, you will do very well. You will start tomorrow in the tea room. I understand from Mr Wilson Beck that you have been used to waiting at tables?'

She did not wait for a reply and ignored Leah's tremulous thanks but turned to Rachel and asked sweetly, 'How is your dear brother? He did not mention his health when he wrote about his friend's daughter. I trust he is in good health?'

Leah stood quietly whilst Rachel and Miss Hartley discussed the handsome grocer. She was overwhelmed with her good luck and already planning to send money to her Mother and to write to Mr Beck to thank him.

'Come here for half past seven tomorrow morning.' Miss Hartley interrupted her reverie. 'You will be given your uniform then. Your wages will be,' she named a sum several shillings more than Leah had earned at the Hall. Leah could not believe her luck. Her feet seemed to float as, after bidding Miss Hartley goodbye, she and Rachel retraced their steps in the busy street and arrived once more at Beck's Groceries.

'You will have to live above the shop,' Rachel explained, 'until we can find you some lodgings. It is just a small room but you can use the room behind the shop for warmth and to make refreshments. I will see you each morning and evening because Beck's opens early to catch passing trade.'

'How can I thank you?' Leah stammered, 'I feel I have never been so fortunate.'

She clasped Rachel's hand.

'I will not let you or your brother down,' she asserted vehemently. 'You have been so kind to me,' her voice faltered and once more she dashed away the tears which fell from her clear eyes down pale cheeks.

'Away with you, Leah,' Rachel protested kindly, 'anyone can see you'll be a good worker. Now settle your things in and we will have a cup of tea. Brian will just have to manage on his own.'

★

True to her word, Leah worked hard. Her job in Miss Hartley's Refreshment Rooms was not, she thought, as hard as had been her job at the Hall. She took pride in her job and enjoyed waiting on the innumerable customers attracted to the shop by its excellent commodities. The other girls liked her, as did Miss Hartley and after a few weeks, Leah felt well, settled and happy. She wrote to her Mother telling her of her luck and the part Wilson Beck had taken to secure this luck and she wrote too to Wilson Beck to thank him for his kindness. Hannah's eyes misted over when she read the letter and on her next foray into Beck's Groceries in Netherghyll she greeted Wilson Beck with an unaccustomed warmth which made a slow blush suffuse his well-shaved features.

All went well for Leah for several weeks until one day she recognised the voices of a couple who had entered the shop. It was Flora Forbes Robertson and Simon Forrester, eager for refreshments after a journey on the Lakes Express.

'A pot of tea and some fresh scones.' She recognised them immediately. Simon had been a frequent visitor to the Hall, rumour had it that he and Flora would marry. Simon was tall and fair with the ruddy complexion of a country man. His family were mine owners and he carried himself with an insolent arrogance. Simon Forrester rapped out the order without bothering even to look up at Leah.

'Yes sir,' Leah averted her face in the hope of avoiding discovery from Flora, but it was too late. Flora's eyes widened and then narrowed as she recognised Leah. As Leah moved away she said something in a low voice to Simon then gave a peal of malicious laughter. Leah's back straightened and she moved away hastily. Useless to think Flora had forgotten her. Leah returned with the tray and deftly placed the crockery and scones on the table. Simon Forrester surveyed her carefully. His eyes moved to her flushed face. Alarm had flooded her face with a pink blush and her eyes were huge, the black of the irises making the clear grey an unexpected contrast. A tendril of white-gold hair peeped through the starched cap and the upswept mass of white showed off her well-shaped head. Her hands, he noticed, having recovered their smoothness now she was no longer sweeping out grates and blackleading ranges, were fine and well shaped. His gaze raked her body, lithe and lissom in her cotton uniform. By God. Here was a beauty. Leah flinched under his gaze.

'Strawberry jam,' Simon Forrester commanded peremptorily as she was about to move from the table, 'you've forgotten the strawberry jam.'

Leah flushed, she knew very well that he had not ordered any jam.

'Yes, sir. At once, sir.' Simon was intrigued with the voice. It was low and well modulated. Almost, he thought to himself, an educated voice. Here was a mystery. He glanced at Flora. Her dark eyes were flashing maliciously as she acknowledged jealously Simon's interest in Leah.

'Come on, Florry,' he said teasingly, 'what's the story? How do you know our little waitress?'

'Little waitress!' Flora replied waspishly, 'why, she is almost as tall as you.' Simon smiled. It excited him to make the proud Flora jealous. She normally treated him with a feigned disdain although it was tacitly acknowledged between them that they would unite their two wealthy families in wedlock. 'She was dismissed from the Hall for seducing my young brother.' Flora embellished the tale of Leah's dismissal with a few hasty words poured out in venom and spite. Words if she had only known aroused Simon Forrester's interest. Leah returned to the table with the strawberry jam. Wordlessly, before she could place the pretty cut glass bowl on the table, he put his hand over Leah's to retrieve it. Leah flinched and pulled her hand away as Simon gave a sly smile at her reaction. Flora's face hardened. She was not going to be ignored for a, she searched for the word, for a slut. When Leah had moved away, she recounted the story of Leah swimming nude under James's fascinated gaze, not realising that her story was provoking a physical reaction in Simon Forrester which he could hardly contain.

In the following weeks, Flora and Simon visited the Refreshment Rooms frequently. Leah began to dread their visits. Although unused to men's attentions, the long, slow considering glances Simon Forrester subjected her to, and the sly smile, as if they were fellow conspirators disturbed her. Whilst Flora's jealous presence dissuaded Simon from making any overt overtures to Leah, yet all the while he was becoming fascinated with her and enjoying the sense of power that Flora's jealousy aroused in him. Leah's cool blonde looks contrasted fiercely with the image he had of her, fanned unwittingly by Flora's spite; she dominated his thoughts and he lay awake at night dreaming of possessing her, or being possessed by her. He imagined her as a passionate and erotic temptress who would succumb to his baser instincts. And then his chance came. Flora was dispatched to an aunt at Chester to accompany her Mother on an extended visit.

'You will behave, Simon?' Flora asked prettily. Jealousy was not an emotion she cared to suffer and although she would not openly acknowledge Simon's interest in Leah, (whey-faced little bitch, she thought nastily,) she knew that her regaling him with the highly embroidered account of Leah's dismissal had aroused his interest. She knew, or she thought she knew, that Simon would not give in to this interest. After all, she thought crossly, it is me who he will marry. But she was wrong. After Flora's departure Simon made every excuse to himself to visit Miss Hartley's Rooms. His Father was pleased that Simon was taking such an interest in the mine at William Pitt that he had to visit Whitehaven so frequently. It excited Simon to have Leah wait on him like a servant, to be so near and yet so far. Leah was aware that he watched her all the time and yet she could find no good excuse not to serve him. One morning Miss Hartley called Leah into her office.

'Leah,' she said 'I want you to know that I am pleased with your work. You are a good worker.' Leah flushed with pleasure and began to thank Miss Hartley. Before she could do so, Miss Hartley interrupted her.

'I have noticed, Leah,' she said somewhat severely, 'that a certain young gentleman is visiting here very often. I would like to think,' she said in a softer tone as she saw Leah's distressed reaction, 'that he is drawn here by the quality of my confection. However, I fear that you, my dear, are the attraction.'

She stopped. Leah's reaction had been so extreme it startled her. Leah's face had paled and the grey eyes filled with tears.

'Oh no, Miss Hartley, no,' she protested. 'I have given him no cause.'

'All I wish to say, Leah,' Miss Hartley continued, 'is do not encourage him. The Forresters are very well respected and influential people. I could not countenance a scandal in my workplace.'

She stopped consideringly; Leah's stricken face had told her all she needed to know and caused her not to revise her original estimate of Leah's character.

'Be careful, my dear,' she concluded warningly.

Leah's mind was in a turmoil. How could she avoid Simon Forrester? His presence in the shop unnerved her, frightened her. However, for a couple of days he did not appear and she was just beginning to feel that maybe his persecution was over when something happened. He was waiting for her after work. The back entrance to the Refreshment Rooms was in a narrow back lane, parallel to the street. Each night the girls changed out of their uniforms and scampered eagerly home down the cobbled passage. It had been a lovely, sunny, blue, early autumn day, a day Leah had only glimpsed in the long hours in the cafe. She was eager to get home, as she now called her little room at the back of Beck's groceries for she and Rachel had promised themselves a walk along the 'Sugar Tongue': to watch the hustle and bustle of harbour life. The small group of girls in front of Leah nudged each other at the sight of Simon leaning nonchalantly against the wall. Although they liked Leah, her education and refinement kept her imperceptibly apart and shop gossip knew that Simon Forrester was waiting for Leah. Leah drew back in dismay as Simon approached her.

'Good evening, Leah,' Simon said softly. His glance surveyed her timid pose which only served to whet his appetite for her.

'What are you doing here,' Leah asked breathlessly, 'why are you here?'

'Why Leah. I do believe you know why I'm here.' Simon replied civilly. 'You have given me plenty of encouragement over these last few weeks.'

'Encouragement?' Leah called out breathlessly, 'I have given you no encouragement.'

'Oh yes you have,' Simon replied savagely, 'just as you gave encouragement to young Master James of Netherghyll Hall.'

'That's a lie,' Leah cried out wildly, 'I gave no encouragement.'

'You call being naked no encouragement?' Simon countered, then mistaking the look on Leah's face, he said quietly, 'Come here, Leah. I mean you no harm. I just wish to be with you for a short while.'

He moved towards her as she shrank away from him and caught her roughly by the arm.

'Come here damn you.'

He jerked her towards him savagely and held her close to him. Leah could feel his body trembling against her and his erection pressed into her, so she tried to pull away even more fiercely.

'Leah.'

Simon arched her body towards him and ran his hands over her body.

'Leah.'

Despite her fear, Leah felt a surge of feeling suffuse her body. He was tall and strong and smelled of cologne. His hands touched her intimately and although she was afraid, they gave her a forbidden pleasure. She was frightened at her own reaction. He groaned and buried his face into her neck as his body convulsively spent himself against her. After a moment he lifted his head.

'No one will believe you, Leah,' he said sombrely. 'Who can you tell? You need a job not another scandal. I will treat you well, give you an allowance, but you must be mine. You shall be mine.'

He released her abruptly and turned and walked swiftly down the lane. Leah was terrified. The imprint of his body lay still against hers, she could taste him on her lips. Her own swift reaction horrified her. Perhaps she was wicked. Yes. Who would believe her? She thought of Wilson Beck and his kindness. He might believe that she was a seductress. She thought of her Mother. How could her Mother stand another scandal? She stood for a long time, her face set and white. Slowly she walked home and made a flimsy excuse to Rachel, who seeing Leah's white-strained face could easily believe in the headache she professed to suffer. The next night he was there again. Leah waited behind after the other girls had gone, hoping that he would tire of waiting for her, but when at last she ventured into the lane he was there.

'Leah.' He moved gracefully towards her. 'You are late, my dear.'

He smiled.

'I thought you had forgotten me?' said Leah bitterly.

'Forgotten you? How could I forget you?' Simon smiled coldly. 'Have you thought about my offer?'

He dragged her unresisting body towards him, pressing her close till she could feel the warmth of his body through her clothes, and the uncontrolled trembling which presaged his release.

'Leah,' he murmured against her hair, 'I must have you. I will have you. I can think of nothing else but possessing you.' He held her closer.

'I can feel your body responding to mine. You know that you would like to be mine.'

'Stop it,' cried Leah wildly, 'I have no feelings for you except disgust that you should treat me so.'

'Ah.' Simon smiled down at her with a dark satisfaction, 'that makes the hunt all the better. You must give me an answer tomorrow Leah. You must consent to be mine. Or,' he looked at her consideringly, 'I shall tell the worthy Miss Hartley that she has a temptress working for her and I shall inform the equally worthy Wilson Beck that the lady who rents his room is a scheming whore. Incidentally,' he asked interestedly, 'does Miss Hartley know why you were dismissed from Netherghyll Hall?'

Seeing her face, he laughed triumphantly, 'I thought not. Now there's a pretty story to tell.'

'Why are you doing this?' Leah asked wildly, 'What have I ever done to make you treat me so?'

'Ah,' he said softly, 'it is what you are *going* to do, dear Leah, which spurs me on. I think of nothing but possessing you...' He stopped consideringly, 'But you must consent to it, Leah. You must say yes or be doubly ruined.'

'What about Miss Flora?' Leah asked quietly. Simon's face darkened.

'Flora? She is a spiteful baggage who intends to marry me. Flora has not served you well and it will be exciting to see her squirm when she knows I have possessed you. Flora will come to heel after a pretty play of pique.' He spoke so dispassionately that Leah shuddered. There was no hope for her. She was trapped. Who would believe her word against that of Simon Forrester.

'Come to me tomorrow, Leah,' he coaxed, 'No. Better still, I will come to Beck's tomorrow night. Another night dreaming of you will whet my... appetite. Leave the door unlocked,' he added menacingly, 'or take the consequences.

I will be a generous master,' he added before turning away and beginning to walk down the alley.

'How do you know I am at Becks?' Leah demanded.

'Leah,' he answered slowly, 'I know everything about you. I know that your Mother is a widow and is broken-hearted at your dismissal from the Hall. But better still,' he smiled rapaciously, his ruddy complexion deepening, 'I know what your mouth tastes like, I know what it will feel like to bury my head in your silken hair and bury my body between your legs. Oh yes, Leah. I know you. I know all about you.'

Leah stared at him aghast, feeling powerless against the passion of his words.

That night she lay awake in the little room she had come to love and call home. What could she do? Where could she go? She thought of succumbing to him. She knew very little about lovemaking but she knew only too well that the trembling uncontrolled man who had spent himself against her did not love her. She thought of her own surprising reaction to the closeness of Simon's body and she blushed bitterly in the darkness. Who would believe her if she said she had given Simon Forrester no encouragement? She thought of her conversation with Miss Hartley. She thought of her Mother's lovely face, haggard with worry and with shame. In the early hours of the morning she made her decision. Dry-eyed, she packed her case. Later she walked to the railway station. She had left no note. If no one knew where she was, Simon Forrester could not follow her. She had a little money. It would not take her very far.

Billy Bowman

Billy Bowman was a king amongst men and he knew it. His green eyes sparkled as he jumped down lightly from his horse and threw the reins to a waiting boy.

'Treat her kindly, lad,' he admonished in a deep melodic voice.

'He has a long way to ga tomorrow.'

For Billy had made the long journey down over the fells from Caldbeck to come to the Martinmas Hiring Fair. Billy Bowman was handsome and part of his effortless charm was the fact that he was completely unaware of his startling good looks. He was tall for a Cumbrian, just over six feet and his skin was brown and smooth, with a russet glow to his cheeks. He was well muscled, for his life was hard on a Cumbrian farm on the Caldbeck Fells. It was his face which commanded attention. His features were classically regular, a long straight nose, high cheekbones, large, firm mouth enclosing white regular teeth topped with a luxuriant glossy moustache, a well defined chin with a roguish dimple, the aforementioned emerald green eyes and black curly, unruly hair tumbling out from under his cloth cap. Billy Bowman did not know he was handsome but he did know that he 'had a way with women'. He treated the eager girls with an offhand good nature and a rough kindness in much the same way he treated his dogs, which only made women flock round him more eager for his attention. For all that, Billy was a 'man's man', popular with his fellows and he had come to Cockermouth this late afternoon to see the sights of the Fair. His intention was to walk round the sights and then sojourn in the Appletree with his mates and then, who knows? A spot of dalliance at the dance with a willing lass perhaps. Billy's green eyes sparkled and he whistled as he walked at the thought of the pleasure to come. Cockermouth's Martinmas Fair was one of the two Hiring Fairs held every six months where those who needed work came from all over the county in the hope of being hired for work. Billy walked round the colourful roundabouts, their gaudily painted horses and animals carrying happily screaming burdens and past the gaily painted swinging boats. Up on the fells, the air had been fresh and sweet as wine but the air in the town was heavy with the sharp smell of sweat and horse dung. A pale sun shone and all was well in Billy's world. He walked on, totally unaware of the admiring glances thrown by sundry young ladies. He picked his way past the large tent where judging by the pleasurable screams, Doctor Biddle's Ghost was frightening half the population. Billy paused and tried his hand at the shooting gallery, enjoying the colour and vitality swirling around him. Skirting the tent which held the 'Pig-faced Woman', Billy passed the Drill Hall. He knew there was dancing there all day and he intended later on to join the merry throng. On an impulse, he walked up Castlegate to see the end of the Hirings. The light was beginning to fade and as the Fair had begun at 5.30 a.m., almost all good strong workers would be hired. Most workers gave indication of their trade by carrying the signature of their work. A blacksmith would carry a hammer, a dairy maid would pin cow's hair to her coat; almost all would give some indication of their anticipated occupation. Billy's attention was caught by the solitary figure of a girl standing dejectedly with her back to him. She was tall but not as tall as he, her back was stooped with weariness and a long strand of flaxen hair hung down from under her straw hat. Intrigued Billy walked over to her.

'What are you selling fair maid?' he asked lightly.

Leah turned slowly at his voice and Billy could see that her face was very pale and her eyes were as grey and cool as a Lakeland mist. Billy looked at her for a long heart-stopping moment, at the cool grey gaze and the transparent honesty in her face and fell instantly and irrevocably in love. His cheeks flushed and his heart hammered in his ears and he had an almost irresistible urge to reach out and touch the white blonde hair which stroked her cheek. When he spoke his voice was husky.

'Sorry maid,' he apologised, 'but are you for hiring?'

'Aye sir,' Leah's voice was low with fatigue. 'I'm looking for a lady to hire me as a maid.'

'And where dost thoo come frae?' Billy was anxious to detain her and was stung with disappointment when the girl answered spiritedly, 'That's not for you to know.' She turned her back on Billy once more but not before he saw a flash of fear pass over her mobile features. Billy shrugged and walked on, he was not used to any female spurning his advances, but his interest in the end of the hirings had gone and he retraced his steps to the Appletree where he was greeted with shouts of welcome from his pals who were already well along the path of drunken enjoyment. Billy had a couple of pints of Jennings good brown ale but his thoughts kept slipping away to the tall girl and her grey gaze and he knew that he must see her again. The Fair finished at 6.30 p.m. and on an impulse Billy made a hurried excuse to his roistering friends and retraced his steps to Castlegate. He often wondered in the years to come what would have happened to Leah had he not done so. His heart leapt with excitement when he saw her standing wearily by her poor suitcase in the gloom. He walked towards her.

'Hey lass,' he said gently, 'the Hirings over. You mun go home now.'

Leah looked at him and the kindness in the bright green eyes touched her heart and all the sights and sounds and events of the day whirled in her head and she swayed dizzily. Billy, greatly daring, touched her arm, 'Have you eaten today lass?' he asked. Leah bit her lip to stop herself crying.

'I... I only have money for a bed for the night,' she answered shakily. Billy picked up he suitcase in a decisive movement.

'Come with me, lass,' he said quietly. Leah was too tired to resist and she walked beside Billy in silence till they came to the Drill Hall where the sounds of the fiddles scraping away for the dancing hung on the frosty air. Billy settled her on a low small wall and went inside, returning after a while with a steaming mug of tea and a hunk of fruit cake. Leah ate gratefully, the warmth of the tea percolating through her tired body.

'There's not much call for ladies' maids round here,' Billy broke the silence, 'thoo'll have to go home tomorrow.'

'I can't,' wailed Leah, all the shame and disgrace she felt welling up in her throat until she felt she could not breathe, until she felt overwhelmed with sadness and a childish desire to be held safe and warm in her Mother's gentle arms and to be held as the child she was.

'I was too late for the Hirings,' she confessed, 'anyway,' she sat up resolutely, 'I thank you, sir, for your kindness. I must away to find lodgings.'

She stood up, and Billy anxious, he knew not why, to detain her said flatly, 'You won't find any lodgings in Cockermouth tonight, they'll all be taken.' Then in desperation at the thought of losing her and his brain in a whirl of inspiration he said, 'Ah was late for the Hirings mesell. We need a maid at the farm to cook and clean. There's only me Father and me and he's getting on.'

Leah looked at him with astonishment, then answered slowly, 'It wouldn't be proper, me and two men.'

'You'd be helping me,' Billy improvised quickly, 'me Father'll murder me if I go back wid no one.' He laughed his delicious laugh, 'he'll know how long ah spent in the pub. Anyway,' he added seriously, 'what can you do? You've nowhere to go. Look,' he said, touched by her evident distress, 'ah'll give you a minute to think it over. Ah'll go for a walk and come back.' Billy walked away without a backward glance, without waiting for her reply, almost overcome with his own audacity. He daren't think what the old man would say, there was no need for anyone at the Farm, they were managing and money was tight enough, although he cheered himself, since his Mother died the previous year, the house had suffered and it would be great to have someone to cook for them. He groaned out loud. He had not asked her if she could cook. Still, the thought of her cool grey gaze slid into his head and he knew with a flash of perception that he would do anything to have the girl near him.

'Are you dancing tonight Billy?' a roguish voice asked and Billy looked down on to the hopeful gaze of a fresh-faced local girl, her face beaming at the thought of a dance with him. He shook her hand absently from his sleeve.

'Not tonight,' he answered shortly.

'Oh, suit yourself,' came the angry reply, 'there's more fish in the sea than you Billy Bowman.' The girl flounced away.

Leah sat still on the wall. She was so tired that she could hardly move or think straight, yet she knew that the stranger's offer was the only thing which stood between her and the Workhouse. She had no illusions. The Hirings were over for another six months. Suddenly she was frightened that he would not return, that his offer had been made lightly and only as an excuse to speak to her. She was in a turmoil and was ready to cry out loud in her misery when out of the gloom she saw Billy's tall figure reappear.

'Can you cook lass?' Billy asked as soon as he was near enough to ask the question.

'Yes,' she answered, somewhat thrown by the unexpectedness of the question, 'and I'm a good strong healthy worker,' she added.

'Is it "yes" then?' Billy asked abruptly. He had been half expecting to find her gone.

'It's "yes",' she answered doubtfully, and stood up. He held out his hand, she noticed it was red and rough unlike the smooth skin of his face.

'Shake to seal the bargain,' he instructed quickly, scared that she might change her mind.

'It's done,' she said firmly, and put her hand in his. He held it tightly, conscious that her hand was already a little rough with work, aware of the blood coursing through his veins and touched by the trust she had placed in him.

For all she knew, he thought, ah could have been a rogue and a vagabond just after her body. He felt incredibly virtuous, a novel experience for him.

'Then you're hired till next Martinmas,' he rejoiced, and dropping her hand, he gave a joyous laugh.

'What's your name lass?' he asked.

'Leah Fletcher,' she answered after a short hesitation, almost feeling that the news of her shame and humiliation would have reached Cockermouth.

'Fletcher?' mused Billy, 'There's Fletchers in Cockermouth.'

'I have no relations in Cockermouth!' answered Leah firmly. Billy questioned her no more. Time enough, he thought, his heightened perceptions recognising that here was a secret, but his instinct told him that the girl was true through and through.

'What's yours?' she asked suddenly. Billy laughed again.

'Billy Bowman,' he replied, relieved that he was not to lose this stranger, half understanding already that he was in the grip of love which only death could extinguish. They walked side by side, not speaking, Leah matching her stride to his long one, back to the Appletree. The Fair surged and swung round them as they walked unheeding of the many curious glances for Billy was a catch hereabouts. The girls cast envious glances at Leah and the men too wondered at the tall girl at his side.

'What's to do then, Billy?' shouted one of his friends as they came to the entrance of the Appletree.

'Are you coming to the Dance? And who's this then?' he asked easily, casting a curious eye at Leah. Billy called for his horse impatiently, waiting for the boy to bring it before he answered.

'This is Miss Leah Fletcher,' he relied as he swung her, still clutching her suitcase on to the broad back of his horse, 'and this is Mr John Bell,' he explained brusquely to Leah. John Bell reached up his hand and as he did so, her hat, already insecurely anchored, fell at his feet and the mass of white blonde hair cascaded over his outstretched hand like a silken river. Billy bent down quickly, unaccustomed jealously piercing his heart.

'Put it on,' he commanded tersely to Leah. Leah did as she was bid, startled at his rough tone as Billy swung himself up behind her.

'Ah have just hired Miss Leah Fletcher to be a maid on our Farm,' he announced grandly, putting his feet to the broad flanks so that the horse set off at a slow canter.

'A maid is it?'

John Bell stood back and scratched his head in amazement.

58

'Well, well,' he sighed happily, 'Billy Bowman's caught at last.'

Soon it was all over Cockermouth that Billy Bowman was taking a girl to Cold Harbour Farm.

The Journey

It was a long and uncomfortable journey but Billy savoured every minute of it. Soon they left the garish sights and sounds and the rancid smells of Cockermouth behind and began the slow climb to the fells of Caldbeck and to the farm. Leah was the first to break the silence.

'What do I call you?' she asked. 'Do I call you sir?'

Billy's joyous laugh splintered the night.

'Nay lass. You call me Billy, and ah'll call you Leah. Ah doan't know what me Father'll call you,' (All the names under the sun he thought apprehensively,) 'but we'll face that when we come to it.' After about half an hour, he suggested tentatively, 'Leah. You'd be better off riding the horse astride than sideways. It's better for the horse, for the weight,' he explained.

'All right,' Leah agreed. Billy stopped the horse with a brisk, 'Whoa lad,' and Leah slipped down on to the stony path. Without a word, she dragged her long skirts between her legs, affording Billy a glimpse of her shapely ankles. Wordless, his throat suddenly dry, he got down and helped Leah to remount, tying her battered suitcase to the saddle bag, then, putting his foot to the stirrup, he swung lightly up behind the girl. As he enfolded her in his arms, reaching the bridle, he felt a rush of piercing happiness overwhelm him. The night was crisp and the length of the lake gleamed mystically like dull silver. Sharp stars spattered the mysterious darkness of the night and a white half moon cut the sky like a sword above the dark silhouettes of the lowering hills. The air was pure and sweet and tinged with a frosty clarity. After a short while, Leah fell into an exhausted sleep. Billy was acutely aware of his body as he had never been before. He felt the slow throb of the horse's steady breathing and the rise and fall of its body between his long legs at each steady step. He felt the scratchiness of his tweed trousers against his thighs and stretched and pushed his feet against the soft wool of his stockings. He felt the coarse linen of his shirt lazily caress his bare chest and the collar of his tweed jacket prickle against his neck. The cool breeze ruffled his dark curls with a seductive whisper. He was aware of the rapid beat of his heart and the blood pounding through his veins. The smooth leather of the reins slipped sensuously between his fingers and he heard each creak and jangle of the harness, each jingle and clink of the brasses, with heightened awareness. The soft breath of the horse steamed out in a ghostly pennant echoed by his and Leah's. Most of all he was aware of the girl in his arms, a sweet burden, the warm rather sweaty odour of her healthy young body mingling with the ripe smell of the horse's hide. The rim of Leah's straw hat teased against his chest and a wayward strand of the white blonde hair, faintly smelling of lavender, insinuated softly against his burning cheek. He was aware of the clothes moulded to her lush, long body, rubbing softly against his and each of his senses registered the warm and pliant contours of her body under the restricting garments. She lay against him in sweet surrender and he held her as close to his beating heart as he dare. Billy knew he would remember this night, this moment, this silver magical landscape as long as he lived.

The night sky was turning a liquid lambent green with the dawn of a new day and the morning star fading from the waking sky, when at last the magic ended.

'Hey lass,' Billy shook the sleeping girl, 'wake up lass. We're home.'

Cold Harbour

Cold Harbour Farm was tucked away in a fold of the Caldbeck Fells. Its name was a corruption from Roman times, for indeed there had been a Roman Road crossing these fells centuries before and the route over Caldbeck still linked Cumberland with Westmoreland and was a main thoroughfare. The farm was long and low, with a straggle of barns surrounding it, it seemed to crouch there like an old dowager spreading her skirts. It was very old, with thick walls and a moss-covered roof. The rising sun caught the mullioned windows and dazzled Leah's eyes. Leah was so stiff she could hardly move. Most of the journey she had dozed against Bill's body, only dimly aware of the circle of his arms. When he swung her down to the ground she stumbled and almost fell so that Billy had to hold her to him for a brief dizzy moment until she recovered her senses. Billy guided her to the hardly used front door, the carved date in stone above the gigantic lintel proclaiming 1681, above which was an inverted horseshoe, a traditional symbol of good luck to the house. Usually the front door was only used for weddings and funerals but Billy somehow felt the moment to be so important that it warranted such solemnity. The massive door creaked protestingly and Leah had to step over the traditional high threshold into the hallen or passage which divided the house in two. The hallen was narrow and gloomy and it took Leah and Billy a moment or two for their eyes to get accustomed to the dim light. Billy guided Leah to a door which led into a large room on the left. Leah stepped in and looked about her in amazement, it was like stepping back in time. A large inglenook enclosed a huge iron range, banked up with glowing embers. Above the range was a wide sandstone mantelpiece littered with old fashioned china, and set into the wall on the right-hand side of the range was an ornately carved wooden cupboard, whilst on each side of the inglenook were two large carved wooden chairs set like rafts on the slate floor. Underneath the two large mullion windows was a huge long low wooden table, so large it must surely have been carved in the room, on each side of which were wooden benches. The back wall of the room was dominated by a huge carved broad cupboard, stretching almost to the ceiling. Two oil lamps hung from thick, smoke-blackened beams on which hung pewter platters. On the floor was a hooky mat. All this Leah took in at a glance at the same time absorbing the general air of neglect and grubbiness in what, although vastly old fashioned, could be a fine room. She did not have long to look about her. A man's shaky voice shouted from an upstairs room.

'Billy? Billy? Is that thoo Billy?' The voice got nearer, 'Eh lad. What's up? I wasn't expecting thee till tomorrow. Ista...' the voice trailed off as its owner entered the room. A tall, well built but decidedly old man, an older version of Billy although the green eyes were faded and the hair white, came stiffly into the room and stopped abruptly at the sight of Leah.

'What's this then?' the old man's voice sharpened in anger. 'What's this lass doing here? Hasta got this lass in trouble Billy?' his rough old voice sharpened in suspicion.

'Nay Father,' said Billy hastily, a flush suffusing the smooth brown skin and the soft Cumbrian dialect thickening, 'watch what thoo's saying. Ah've,' he paused then the words came out in a rush. 'Ah've hired her to be our maid.'

'Hired her?' The old man's voice lifted incredulously. 'Hired her? As what our Billy? What would thoo want wid a maid? Hasta hired her to be your fancy woman thoo means? To be your fancy woman? Aye a fancy woman mair like. What use do the likes of us have for a maid?'

Billy took a step forward in anger and raised his voice.

'Quiet Father. Ah've fetched Leah here to be our maid. She's not my fancy woman.'

His Father interrupted, 'Leah? A fine to do. Your Mother will turn in her grave.'

'Father,' said Billy loudly, 'this is Miss Leah Fletcher. Ah hired her at Cockermouth Fair. She had nowhere to go and no money and ah thowt we could use someone to… look after us.'

'Nowhere to go! No money! Eh lad, she's seen you coming. This 'un's no better than she should be ah'll be bound.' His Father countered savagely. Leah stood, trembling at the raised voices, the enormity of her situation impinging on her tired brain. Shakily she turned to Billy.

'Billy,' she asked him imploringly, 'tell him it's true you've hired me. Tell him I'm to be a maid here until next Martinmas. It is true isn't it?' her voice trailed off in exhaustion.

'It's true Father. Ah'll find the money for her somehow. Ah'll go without for her.' Billy sprang to the carved cupboard in the wall and swiftly wrenched out a large Bible.

'Ah swear on our family Bible that ah've hired Leah Fletcher till next Martinmas and,' he paused, knowing that the words he was about to say had an almost mystical importance, 'and ah swear on the Holy Bible that ah will protect Leah Fletcher and not lay a hand on her and that,' he felt his heart wrench at the words, 'she will be free to go before the Hiring Fair next Martinmas – if she wants.' He stopped and looked at his Father with an unspoken plea in his green eyes, his body turned to him imploringly. His Father looked at him, this boy his mirror image, and realised with a pang that this unknown girl was somehow important to Billy, that she had, he thought 'cast a spell on him' to make him swear such an oath. He nodded his head slowly.

'Aye well, Billy,' he said quietly, 'that's a gey strong oath and ah respect you for mekking it. Now then lass,' he turned to Leah, 'tell me where you come from and who ye be?'

Leah turned to him slowly and turned her level grey gaze on him.

'Mr Bowman,' she said pleadingly, 'what your son says is true. I was too late for the Hirings and I had only money for a night's lodgings. We shook hands on the hiring.' Her voice began to quiver. 'I'll work hard for you Mr Bowman. I'm a good strong worker and I'm an honest God fearing girl.' She swayed and put her hand out to the old man. He looked at her consideringly. He was astute and a good judge of character and he was impressed at the sincerity in her voice. He stretched out his large weather-beaten hand, rough and leathery.

'Right lass,' he said almost gently, 'right lass, Leah isn't it? You're welcome lass.'

He turned to Billy briskly.

'Get you gone and see to that horse of yours, and you lass, sit you down by the fire and ah'll mek a cup of tea and thoo can tell me all aboot Miss Leah Fletcher.'

The Farm

Leah woke in the late afternoon. At first, in her half waking she thought the room was on fire. On struggling into consciousness, she realised it was the rays of the setting sun which were flaring through the large dusty window and colouring the whitewashed walls. She lay for a while thinking about the events of the previous day. Billy and his Father had decided that until a bed be got ready for her, she should sleep in Billy's room, so now she lay in Billy's narrow iron bed. The deep feather mattress was moulded to the shape of Billy's long body and the bedclothes, for there had been no time to change them, smelled of Billy. She turned her head on the bolster where Billy's head had lain only the day before. It was a not unpleasant smell, more a healthy warm spicy smell. She pushed the thought away from her; Billy Bowman might be her saviour but she wanted nothing to do with him. Men and their lusts would not hurt her again. Slowly, she looked round the room. In a corner stood a small pine wardrobe with a drawer underneath, an old silvered mirror was fixed to the door. A rather fine mahogany chest of drawers stood against one wall on which was a photograph in a wooden frame. A rocking chair with a faded pink plush seat completed the furniture apart from a small nondescript wooden table next to the bed on which was a china rose patterned candlestick. The floor was bare except for a hooky rug at the side of the bed. She stretched her body luxuriously in the cosy warmth of the bed and unexpectedly, with the languid movement of her body, the thought of James's drawings flooded into her brain and of Simon Forrester's hard body close to hers, and the familiar feelings of shame and disgrace rose up in her heart. Frantically, she pushed aside the sheets and faded patchwork quilt and went to the open window. She pushed it open to its fullest extent, absently noticing the dust smeared on the old green glass, and leaned out of the window. The view made her catch her breath. Far below, over the moors, gilded by the setting sun lay the Plain of Carlisle sweeping out towards the Solway, the sea glittering crimson in the evening light, whilst due west the clouds banked up, purple and rose, black and grey, scarlet and fuchsia, spreading and unfolding in a towering panoply of majesty. Leah stood and gazed, awed and moved by the sight and the glory of the sunset. Her sorrows seemed to fade far away and she stood in her bare feet watching the ever changing scene whilst the light faded imperceptibly. The air was sharp and with a slight shudder she started to put on her clothes before the light went completely. With a wry smile she tied on her coarse apron and put on the steel-tipped clogs. Pulling up the bed clothes, her eye was caught by the photograph on the chest of drawers. It framed the picture of a handsome woman with laughing eyes, presumably Billy's Mother. She thought of her own dear Mother and her heart sank again and tears came to her eyes. She stopped and looked at herself in the silvery mirror, its blotched and worn surface reflecting her pale face. Swiftly she braided her hair into a thick plait and then looked at herself intently. Her reflection was one of total dejection. Proudly she lifted her head, her grey eyes suddenly cold with resolution. She squared her shoulders under the rough serge of her dress and muttered, 'Only a year, Leah, only a year. Make the most of it lass,' then she turned and went out on to the landing. Billy's room and his Father's room were on each side of an outer landing, in the middle was an opening topped by a huge beam which led into an inner landing. She dimly remembered the old man saying that the bathroom was 'Inby' so she went through the arch into the corridor. To the right was another bedroom and to the left the bathroom, a cold echoy room with a huge bath on clawed feet and a large white basin with brass taps. Leah guessed that the privy would be outside as it was in most houses. She walked back to the main landing and then clattered down the slate steps to the hallen. Opening a door to her left she found the dairy, a small cavernous room. Stone shelves lining the walls held an assortment of bottled preserves and on a long pine table were jugs of milk, a bowl of cream, some cheese and butter. She closed the door and went further along the hallen to the next room which was obviously a store room. Turning back she went into the large room where she had met Billy's Father. The banked up range bubbled and squeaked comfortably and she stood for a moment warming herself before she noticed another door in the corner of the room. This led into the kitchen. A large pine dresser held an assortment of dusty china and in the large white pot sink under the window was a pile of unwashed dishes. The window looked out on to a cobbled yard with byres and stables. There was no sign of life. With a grimace of distaste at the pile of dishes Leah tightened her apron and began her first task as maid at Cold Harbour Farm.

Billy too had been watching the sunset. The sheep were being brought down from the high fells and soon, at the end of November, the tups or rams would be put to the ewes for the age old circle of renewal to begin. He was a simple man and like all simple men, extremely complicated. On the farm, Billy was involved in the continual mystery of birth and death, growth and renewal but if you had asked him if he was a religious man he would have answered, no. He did go to church but only as a habit, enjoying it for the familiar custom and company. Yet Billy Bowman was a spiritual man, he found his God on the high fells when he was alone in the shining air. His inner conviction was that his God was the God of the twenty-third psalm, and he often murmured the well-loved words to himself when he was shepherding his sheep, 'The Lord is my shepherd', but Billy's God was a solitary God and a personal God and he would have laughed his jolly laugh in embarrassment if anyone had said he was a spiritual man, his lack of education hampering his explanation. Yet tonight Billy looked into the setting sun, glorying in its savage beauty, aware that his simple life had changed and yet he knew not how. He thought of the vow that he had made to the girl, that he would protect her, aye that he would, and that he would not lay a hand on her. He smiled quizzically to himself. That vow would be hard to keep, his instinct was to hold her to him, caress the smooth pale skin, to kiss the grey eyes and, oh, to let down that pale white hair. His pulses raced at the thought of her, her proud stance, the way she held her head, the small work-worn hand in his. Yet Billy was a farmer and his farming instinct told him that here was someone hurt and damaged, by what he knew not, but he resolved he would use all his patience and kindness to keep Leah Fletcher in this place, his place, to be his own. By God, he thought, it'll be hard seeing her everyday, wanting that young body close to mine, to be mine, but as God is my witness, he looked towards the setting sun, I'll keep my vow.

Cold Harbour Farm was a sheep farm, farming the Herdwick. The wool of the Herdwick was coarse but the sheep could withstand exposure better than other breeds. Its origins were shrouded with mystery. Some said that the breed originated from forty or so animals washed ashore on the Cumberland coast at the time of the Armada; some said that the sheep originated in Scandinavia, but the Herdwick were ideal for the Caldbeck Fells, able to live up to two weeks buried in a snowdrift and with a particular homing instinct for their own pasture which made them unique. The ageless cycle of gathering, lambing, dipping and clipping ruled Billy and his Father's lives as it had done their forefathers for centuries.

Leah, Billy and the old man, sat in the cavernous depth of the living room, close to the comforting range. They had discussed what duties Leah should do, which were mainly in the house. She was to sleep in the room next to the bathroom which overlooked the yard, stables and barns. Tomorrow was Sunday and the old man had demanded that she accompany Billy and he to church.

'Does a maid go to church?' asked Leah timidly, for to tell the truth she had no desire to be yet again the target of curious eyes.

'Aye, she does,' agreed the old man firmly, 'twice a day. And the sooner the villagers see you, the sooner they'll get used to you, lass. You've nowt to hide and neither have we.'

Leah felt cheered by this comment but next morning when they walked down the steep path into Caldbeck her heart fluttered in panic and she would have given anything to have evaded the ordeal. Caldbeck had once been a thriving village with a bobbin mill and weaving sheds when the wool industry had been at its zenith. However, now with cheap imports of ready made clothes the industry had declined and many people no longer dressed in the hodden, the cloth made from the hardy brown and white Herdwick sheep, and the bobbin mill was silent as was the weaving sheds and the cottage industry of weaving at home had ceased. It was now no more than a straggle of houses, a flour mill, a pub, The Oddfellows, and a very fine church and vicarage. Leah had no desire to look about her but she was struck by the loveliness of the old church.

'There's bin a holy place here for hundreds of years,' explained the old man, 'there was a hospice here for wayfarers in the twelve hundreds.'

They entered the church and sat down towards the front of the church.

'They'll get a good look at us,' said the old man wisely. Leah's wounded spirits were soothed by the place, the air of tranquillity, the continuity of worship and the simple explanation of the scriptures by the small balding vicar. She joined in the hymn singing and Billy looked sideways at her as she sang in a clear high voice. At the end of the service when they walked outside into the morning sun, the vicar, the Reverend Bray spoke to the three of them and the old man introduced Leah as 'Miss Leah Fletcher, our maid,' in a voice loud enough for any eavesdroppers to hear a mile off and fierce enough for no one to disagree. The vicar greeted her cordially and shook her hand.

'And where are you from Leah?' he asked. Billy sensed Leah stiffening.

'Oh, from the west of Cumberland,' she replied quickly and walked on up the path without waiting for a further question. Of course there was talk in Caldbeck, there is always talk in small villages, but the old man's introduction and the vicar's handshake lent Leah a welcome air of respectability. They made the long walk to and from the church in the evening when the fells were flaming red in the fading sun.

'You see Leah,' Billy explained, 'when the snows are here, we can't get down to the church.' Leah nodded but could not imagine being snowed in.

November was the time when the sheep were brought down from the high fells for the winter so Billy and his Father were out from dawn to dusk, coming in at night to stretch their long legs before the fire. Leah worked in the house. She was determined to clean the house systematically and started on the small scullery first, scouring it till it gleamed and sparkled. Three days after her arrival she presented a list to Billy. She had searched the house for paper and found only a torn envelope and a stub of pencil.

'Billy, if I am to keep the house clean these are the things I must buy. Do you agree to my list?'

She handed the torn scrap of paper to Billy who took it automatically. He studied it and twisted it in his hands in agitation, a flush rising in his brown face.

'You'll have to read it to me,' he said after a long silence and the colour bloomed in his cheeks, 'I… cannot read, Leah,' he mumbled and turned away. Leah looked at him, at this great handsome man who did not have the advantage of a small child in an elementary school.

'It's no matter, Billy,' she said matter-of-factly, taking the scrap of paper from him gently, 'I'll read it for you.'

There was some discussion as to the contents of the list and when agreement was reached, Leah asked nervously, 'Please could I buy some writing paper and ink and some stamps so that I may write to my Mother?'

She now knew why she could not find any in the house.

'Aye, lass,' said Billy's Father kindly, 'Billy and me has talked and we're going to advance you a laal bit of your wages so that thou has summat for thisen and we'll give you summat each week for the shopping.'

The next day Leah walked down the long path to the village. This time she stopped and looked around her at the wonderful scenery. Far away in the clear cold light, Skiddaw dominated the skyline majestically, the hills around it folding and unfolding in a dizzy panorama of blues and greys which seemed to never end. Leah put down her basket and gazed and gazed. Coming from a coastal town she had seen the great banks of the Lakeland mountains always at a distance but to be so close to all the raw power of the mountains and to feel so small in comparison moved her immensely. There was not a sound and the shifting purple clouds formed and reformed in wraith-like beauty. Far above, a buzzard wheeled and turned in the chill sun, twisting and turning in the clear air. She felt cleansed and for one brief moment she felt at one with all the elements of her surroundings, as if she had found her right place. She stood until the chill November air roused her, and picking up her basket she moved on down the path to the village.

Letters

Cold Harbour Farm,
Caldbeck

My dearest Mother,

You will see by my address where I am residing. I am sorry if my hurried departure from Whitehaven caused you sorrow but I could no longer stay there and endure the gossip. (She did not tell her Mother of Flora's part in her departure or the brutal advances made to her by Simon Forrester.) *There were other reasons too which I will tell you when we meet again... soon I hope, dear Mother. I was hired at the Martinmas Fair in Cockermouth to become a maid for Cold Harbour Farm on Caldbeck, see address above. The family are kind* (she omitted to write that the family consisted of Billy and his Father). *I have been hired for a year. Believe me, dear Mother, I am being well treated. I am to look after the farmhouse, to clean and cook. What a good job, dear Mother, that you taught me to cook and that Mrs Hodgson at the Hall often asked me to help her and of course, dear Mother, I am no stranger to cleaning! Caldbeck means cold water river, so Mr Bowman, the farmer, tells me. They are kind to me and I am well.*

I love you dearest Mother. I will save all my money so that I may come and see you in six months time. I always think of you and miss you so much but please do not worry about me as I am well. I send you, dearest Mother, all my

*love and I hope that you will be able to write to me soon,
your ever loving daughter,*

    Leah

*P.S. As I told you, I am hired here for a year. Maybe after
this year I can return to you, dearest Mother, and the talk
will have died down. One day, dear Mother, one day...*

                        *Ghyllside lodge,
Netherghyll
Whitehaven*

Dearest child,

    *I was overjoyed to receive you letter and to know that you
are safe. I have been faint with worry to know where you are.
Rachel Beck told me of your great distress. How I longed to
hold you close to me to shield you from such indignity. I am
outraged that you should be treated so. Yes, you are right
Leah, when you vow 'one day, one day.' Let us say that to
ourselves like a talisman. I am sure that one day we will be
together to live happily.*

    *Meanwhile let us resolve to face life as we always have,
with hope and good humour. I am teaching again at the
school, the children are very slow and have frequent absences
for trivial reasons but I am content.*

    *Lizzie from the Hall gave me this package. I do not
know what it contains! She was very mysterious as if we
shared a secret. Pray tell me Leah when you next write what
it contains.*

    I send you all my thoughts my child,

    *Love and kisses,
Mother*

P.S. Mr Beck has taken to walking his dog as far as the lodge some nights. He always visits to enquire after your welfare.

Leah examined the package carefully but the paper gave no clue to its contents. Tearing the paper slowly she pulled out a folded letter. On opening it she found inside three five pound notes. She looked at them in amazement and then unfolded the letter.

I do not know your name, the letter read, written in Taylor's fine hand *but I am outraged at the way you have been treated at the Hall. I know from your attention to the conversations which took place between me and the Captain of your interest in the world around you. I beg you please accept this money. It is nothing to me, I am rich but I have given it to you for a specific purpose. Regard it as the talents in the Bible and use it wisely for your education, for with education comes freedom. If you can read, buy books to educate yourself, if you cannot read pay someone to teach you but I beg you do not be proud and feel you cannot accept it. I beg you use it to some purpose.*

It was signed by Taylor O'Neill. There was the address of a Liverpool shipping agent at the bottom of the letter.

Leah sat for a long time looking at the money. It represented two years wages. How different her life might have been if she had only remained at Whitehaven. The money would have given her time to plan her future. She sighed and then remembering the fright she had felt at Simon Forrester's advances she felt that she had done the only thing possible. She held the letter in her hand carefully and then read and reread it. She had felt an affinity with the fiery American and had sometimes felt when Taylor and the Captain had conversed so freely in the breakfast room that he was indirectly directing his thoughts and conversation to her, she had then dismissed these ideas as fanciful. The letter confirmed her instincts. Taylor O'Neill, probably thousands of miles away now, had thought of her with kindness and inspiration. The thought warmed her in her loneliness and she determined to fulfil the obligation the money had put upon her.

★

Cold Harbour Farm,
Caldbeck

Dear Mr O'Neill,
  I am indebted to you for the chance you have given me and I will use the money for the purpose it was intended, it will change my life one day I am sure. I am at present working as a hired maid on Caldbeck…

Leah started describing the farm and the loneliness and solitude of the fells and its beauty. Her pen scratched over the paper telling him of the isolated village and the old Roman road over the fells. She told him of the farmhouse and its age and far away in America, many years later when the letter finally reached Taylor at the end of his voyaging, her words were so alive that he could shut his eyes and see again the cool grey gaze of the little kitchen maid and the white blonde hair peeping from under her cotton cap.

★

Billy's Father, like all farmers, could read the weather like a book. One day towards the end of December, he came into the kitchen and said to Leah, 'Snow's coming, Leah. Thoo'd best put some provisions by because when it does thou won't be gaan till the village much.'

Leah looked at him in amazement. It was unseasonably mild, the sky was a voluptuous gold and the air warm.

'Snow?' she repeated, 'but the weather is lovely.'

'Ah tell you lass, it's gaan to snow,' the old man repeated, 'ah can tell the signs.'

Billy agreed with the old man that night.

'We'd best get stocked up, lass,' he said, 'Father allas knows. Ah tell you what, ah'm going to Wigton tomorrow to the auction. You can come with me... if thou likes,' he added shyly.

Leah agreed with enthusiasm, she had not been far in her short life and it would be good to get away from the farm and Caldbeck although she loved the wide open spaces.

They set off in the pony and trap early the next morning; the day was bright and still unseasonably warm. Leah had taken some of Taylor O'Neill's money as she had not yet got her advance on her wages and was too shy to ask for them since she had been at the farm for such a short time. Christmas was coming and she wanted to buy presents for her Mother, Billy and his Father. The journey to Wigton entranced Leah. There was not much conversation between her and Billy; she was too busy looking around her. Billy whistled a happy tune. His world was complete, he had Leah by his side and all was well with the world. They bowled down the hill into Wigton and Billy pulled the horse to a stop at the meeting cross of the little market town.

'Ah'll meet thee in an hour, Leah,' he said, 'will thou be all right?'

He came round to the side of the trap and swung Leah down in his arms.

'Yes, Billy, of course,' Leah replied joyously, pleased that he was not to accompany her on her errands or expect her to go to the auction.

'Just give the grocers the list of provisions,' added Billy before he drove off, 'and ah'll collect them before ah pick thou up.'

Leah was entranced. The little market town was full of country folk and the market stalls were bustling. Having given her list to the grocers she could concentrate on herself alone. What luxury. On an impulse she bought herself a fine grey shawl which she slung round her shoulders. Cold Harbour Farm was draughty and if the snow came she had no other clothes than those she possessed and which she wore all the time. She bought a fine red wool scarf for her Mother, thinking how well it would go with her Mother's colouring. Then she bought separate purchases for Billy and his Father. She bought a copy of *Great Expectations* and *Jane Eyre* in a small dusty bookshop. The church clock was striking three when she stood at the market cross waiting for Billy. She felt no constraint with him, daily contact had rubbed away any embarrassment and most of the time he was out on the fells whilst she worked in the farm and although most afternoons she walked for a while before returning to make the evening meal their paths had never crossed.

She stood waiting, her face bright with excitement, the grey shawl round her shoulders accentuating her lovely eyes and the unaccustomed enjoyment had brought colour to her normally pale cheeks. She attracted many admiring glances as she stood bareheaded in the winter sun. Billy thought he had never seen anything as lovely as the sight of her standing waiting for him alone and a great surge of happiness flooded through him. His delight was somewhat dampened when he saw the packages in her arms and realised that the fine grey shawl was new. Where, he wondered miserably had Leah got the money to pay for the packages and the shawl? If she had money where had she got it from? He knew that Leah had not received any money from him or his Father and had looked forward to surprising her with some before their return home. She had told him at the Martinmas Fair that all she had was money for her lodgings. That was it. His brow cleared. She must have used the money for the lodgings. Truth to tell, Leah felt a trifle guilty about using Taylor's money, even though she had bought some books but she was young and she consoled herself that she would save her wages till next Martinmas Fair when she would leave Caldbeck. So deep in thought was she that the pony and trap were beside her for a moment before she realised they were there and she looked up with a start to see Billy looking down at her intently. It was as if, being away from him for a while, she was seeing him for the first time and she felt the impact of his astonishing good looks. The sunlight glinted on his luxuriant black curls and his green eyes sparkled at her in greeting. She caught her breath for something in his gaze, a warmth, a depth stirred something inside her and for a long moment they looked at each other, openly and without guile, green eyes meeting grey, then both looked away whilst a slow blush consumed their cheeks.

'Hasta had a good time, Leah?' Billy asked after he had helped her into the trap and they were on their way up the long climb to Caldbeck.

'It was wonderful Billy,' Leah thanked him gratefully. 'I enjoyed every minute.'

The conversation flowed easily and Billy made Leah laugh with his descriptions of some of the farmers at the auction. It was the first time that Billy felt completely at ease in her presence. Having her so close had been heaven and hell and the memory of his mighty oath had constrained his natural charm. Now, in the sunshine, with

Leah at his side and the miles home to look forward to, the warmth and attraction of his personality was magnetic. Leah suddenly felt no constraints with him and relaxed under his sincerity. The pain of her betrayal by James and her treatment by Simon Forrester was lessening and her natural optimism returning. They chattered together like two children let out of school.

She asked him openly why he had never learned to read and he replied candidly without embarrassment.

'When you're a farmer's only lad Leah, there's nivver a good time to ga to school. In the winter you're snowed in, in the spring you're lambing, in the summer you're sheering and in the autumn you're moving them down till the low fells, and,' he looked at her engagingly, 'that was allus a queer sight more interesting than gaan to school.' He laughed his joyous infectious laugh and Leah joined in too and felt again that jolt of amazement at Billy's unselfconscious attraction.

Billy's Father watched them sitting close together as the trap turned into the yard. He was struck by their good looks and the contrast between blonde and dark. He watched as Billy swung Leah down from the trap and how Billy's hands lingered on Leah's slim waist and how, unconsciously, Leah leaned towards Billy. So that was the way of it. He'd have to have a word with that young fool. Anyone could see that that was an educated lass and not for the likes of Billy. He could see Billy making a fool of himself over the lass. She'd break his heart and then leave him. Nay, she was not the lass for Billy.

Winter

The snow came early. Leah woke one morning to find the inside of her window covered with ice and a thin grey light filtering into her room. Scraping a space in the scrolls and whorls of frost, she looked out. The whole world was white and large gusts of snowflakes were whirling over the yard. After washing and dressing, she hurried downstairs, along the hallen, to open the front door to see the snow. She was unable to move it and when she went through to the living room she looked out of the window to see that the snow was already piled up as high as the sills. It was like being in an underground cave, the whole world was white and eerie. Billy, his Father and Leah were like hibernating animals. Their life seemed to revolve round the hearth as people had in Northern climes for years.

'Folk tell that some fires burned for centuries in the old days,' Billy's Father told Leah, 'they used to say that when the fire goes out t'soul goes out of t'people in t'house.' Leah could believe it and at the end of the short working day, when all chores were done they sat down companionably before the glowing fire. Almost like a family, thought Billy happily. He liked to look across at Leah as she was busy at some task. One night it was so cold in her bedroom that Leah brought her book downstairs. She had begun to read *Great Expectations* and despite her enjoyment it was too cold in her bedroom to stay up above the covers and read by the light of the oil lamp. Billy watched her read for a couple of nights then one night he asked suddenly, urgency in his voice, 'Leah? Will you read till us?'

Startled, Leah looked up from her book and seeing the anguish in his face lest she refuse, she said quietly, 'Of course, Billy.'

The nightly reading became habitual and even the old man began to enjoy listening to Leah's expressive voice unfolding the story. The old man had spoken to Billy severely after the trip to Wigton.

'She's not for thee Billy. Yon's an educated lass. She won't stay ah'm telling you. Don't git involved,' he warned. Billy had rounded on him fiercely.

'Ah made my vow Father and ah've kept it. Ah haven't laid a finger on her and neither ah will. That's all there is to say. Ah said she'll go at Martinmas and that she will.'

Yet still his heart yearned towards her. She had made the house a home, he glanced round the fine room, polished and shining in the firelight and he hungered to keep her here. He loved everything about her, her voice, her hair, her looks, but now living near her he knew she was kind and hard-working; he loved her, whatever secrets she might have. Billy knew she had secrets for each week now, since the snow had come, she brought her writing things downstairs and wrote at the long table. He had seen that she wrote two letters, one he reasoned would be to her Mother. He knew she had no other relations for he had asked her point blank one day and he tortured himself with wondering to whom Leah wrote so assiduously each week and yet he knew he had no business to ask her.

Christmas Day came and still the snow kept its icy grip. Billy and his Father had roamed the fells each day to rescue sheep caught in the huge drifts and were out with the dogs until dusk. The old man had brought a twist of holly to decorate the beams, for holly had a long remembered far-off mystic significance in the cloistered fells. Leah had cooked a goose; it had been hanging behind the kitchen door for the last week, and she had also managed to make a creditable Christmas pudding and that night they sat round the big table until at last, replete, they sat in satiated silence.

'Eh, Leah lass, that was grand!' said the old man, 'almost as good as Billy's Mother used to mekk.'

'Better ah think,' murmured Billy quietly. Leah got up and went to the large sandstone mantelpiece and came back with two packages, the purchases she had made in Wigton.

'These are for you,' she said shyly, handing them to the two men. 'Happy Christmas.'

The old man's package contained tobacco and a new slender pipe which he immediately began to make up with cries of pleasure. Billy opened his and sat back in amazement.

'What's this then Leah?' he asked. Inside were some child's exercise books and some pencils and a dictionary, 'What's this then?'

'I'm going to teach you to read,' said Leah happily, 'and then when I'm gone you can read to your Father or for yourself.' The remark hung in the air like a sword between them and pierced Billy to the heart.

Aye, he thought, she'll go. She doesn't think ah'm good enough for her either. A small spark of anger invaded him, ah'll show her, he thought, ah'll read. If she can I can. He thanked her gravely and said, 'Aye, well tomorrow mebbe you'll give me the first lesson?' The old man broke the tension between them.

'We have a present for you lass, but thoo'll have to keep it in the byre.' He went out of the door to the hallen and came back a few minutes later with a small wriggling black and white puppy, a sheepdog.

'Oh,' Leah felt the tears rising in her eyes and she bent and buried her head in the small warm licking bundle, 'oh, this is the best present I've ever had!' and the tears spilled over and down her cheeks. She thought of her Mother, alone, wondering what sort of Christmas she would be having, if the scarf had reached her and suddenly she wanted her more than anything in the world, wanted that unconditional love to enfold her and to be home instead of in this old farmhouse with two strangers. Billy and his Father looked away in embarrassment at her emotion but both were touched by the gentle tears.

And so began the pattern which was to last through the winter months. Each night after the evening meal, Leah and Billy sat at the long table and Leah taught Billy to read and write. The old man sat and smoked his pipe and warmed himself by the fire, looking at the fair head and the dark bent over the books in deep concentration. The puppy, now called Holly, sat at Leah's feet. It would not endure being parted from her and any attempt to put it out in the byre with the other dogs was resisted with loud howls and moans. Billy's Father knew the world was changing, even in his little sheltered remote part of the world, and he knew that he must move with it.

Ah well, he thought sadly, what must be must be. He had never needed to read and write, his handshake had been enough to seal a bargain. He looked at Leah and Billy and wondered what changes they would see and what would become of them. He feared that his loving, laughing careless son would be humiliated and hurt by the stranger who had arrived in their midst.

It was in those dark and fire-rosy evenings that Leah began to love Billy. She loved him not with a physical passion at first but gently, sweetly as a Mother loves a child. She watched him struggling over his letters, the good-looking face tense with determination, the dark curls falling over his green eyes, his tongue held between the white teeth. She loved him because of his country innocence and because every day his innate sharp intelligence was making sense of the meaningless black squiggles on the pages of a child's exercise book. She loved him because he was trying so hard and she loved him because he was Billy and his warmth and generosity came shining through in his face. She loved him because he tried so hard to please her. She knew that Billy could read the fells and the clouds and the shift in wind as easily as she could read a book and she wanted to open up a new world which was closed to him where he could move in his imagination as swiftly as he did on the fells. She watched him and she began to love him. She thought of Taylor, telling her that education was the key. She still wrote to him each week, and all the time she wrote to him she never knew, or would have cared that her letters were piling up unread in the dusty shipping office, unsold after the agent's death. Her letters to Taylor became her diary, and in them she wrote of her loneliness, about her life amongst the fells and of her unspoken unacknowledged growing love for Billy. Neither did Taylor wonder about her or even give her a thought because he was working hard in the New World to amass his fortune before the clouds of war broke open and spilled death upon the world. Thoughts of the little kitchen maid at Netherghyll Hall had long vanished from his mind.

The snows lingered amongst the hills well into February when the sheep were gathered off the hills for dipping to guard against lice and keds which could seriously damage the flock, and at the beginning of March, Billy and the old man brought them to the 'inland' pasture where the lambs would be dropped from the middle of April until the middle of May. The intimacy of the winter was over, the days grew longer and the air grew invigorating with a fresh excitement that the winter was nearly coming to an end. It was a hard and arduous time and the two men had to use all their store of veterinary skills. After the dark days of winter, Leah gloried in the surge of light and the high skies. She began to clean the house from top to bottom, throwing open the closed up windows to let in the fresh sparkling air, and she began to resume her walks on the fells. Her trips into the village were ordeals no longer and she enjoyed a leisurely chat in the village shop or conversations with the worshippers at church. And yet there was a restlessness in her like an itch she could not scratch. She wanted something but she knew not what. A vague unspecified longing grew in her, some days a desire to move away from the constricting hills almost overcame her, and then she felt as if she never wanted to move away from the farm and Caldbeck and the mountains and her spirit told her that she was in the right place. All the time there was Billy. She watched him, gentle with a Motherless lamb in his strong rough hands or whistling up his dogs, cuffing them playfully as they sprang eagerly to him and she wondered secretly what his hands would feel like holding her gently, close to him. One day she stood in her bedroom and watched him in the yard strip off his muddy shirt and thrust his curly head under the old pump, laughing out loud as the cold stream of water cascaded over his back. She looked at his body, tall and slim and well-muscled, at the shape of his head under the slicked back hair, at his long strong legs taut against his britches and she shivered deliciously and a longing for she knew not what delight grew in her body. She missed their nights of intimacy when they had sat together at the long table and yet she was glad to be away from him with the thought that she could, she would, go at Martinmas.

Then suddenly things changed. She had noticed in her Mother's frequent letters that the name of the handsome grocer Mr Beck was getting frequently mentioned but she was still not prepared for the shock of her Mother's letter.

Ghyllside Lodge,
Ghyllside

Dearest Child,

My dear friend Wilson Beck has asked me to be his wife and I have accepted. I have been so lonely without you my dear child and Wilson has filled a corner of my heart with his kindness and concern.

Wilson's business has done well of late and he has opened a new shop in Workington. We will live there when we are married and Wilson will leave a manager in the shop at Ghyllside. I hope that you will be happy for me Leah. It is a long time since our Father died and I have great affection for my dear Wilson. We will marry at Martinmas when you come home and you will be able to live with us. Wilson will give you a job, of course. Please write soon and let me know your feelings.

Your loving Mother

Leah read and reread the letter. She felt lost and cut adrift, orphaned from the person she loved and longed for. She thought of the shopkeeper and felt supplanted in her Mother's affections, she thought of living in Workington and working in a shop when she had this glorious freedom and cathedral-like space to live in. That afternoon when she went out for her walk with Holly, she took the letter from her pocket and read it again. Tears filled her eyes and ran down her cheeks and she sobbed aloud for the loss of her childhood, for the loss of her Mother, for never again being first in her Mother's affections, although she knew her Mother loved her dearly. The dog at her feet looked up at her anxiously and nuzzled her skirt but Leah cried only more for a longing for affection and comfort. She felt like Ruth in an alien land, dispossessed and homeless. She was like that when Billy found her.

'Leah lass. Leah,' he cried, horrified to see her distress, 'what's the matter? Are you hurt?' He came towards her and obeying an impulse he could not deny put his arms gently round her, and at last, oh at last, he gently smoothed her pale blonde hair. Leah turned her face into his rough jacket and sobbed even harder and found herself held even tighter.

'Tell me lass,' Billy demanded urgently. 'Tell me what's wrong,' and Leah found herself telling him everything, her dismissal from the Hall, her stay in Whitehaven, Simon Forrester's unwelcome attentions and her Mother's impending marriage. Billy couldn't make sense of it all and when he questioned her again and learned the reason for her dismissal from the Hall his jaw tightened. Leah, his Leah, swimming naked for all to see, and drawn for some smutty gentry to paw over. Imperceptibly he drew away from her and his arms slackened, he was shocked by the story. He had thought her to be pure and unsullied, untouched by any man, even any man's lewd thoughts. He thought of Simon Forrester touching her and his jaw clenched. Leah felt him move away from her and instinctively knew his thoughts.

'You are just the same!' she cried wildly, 'You don't think of how I felt, a child swimming in a secret place on a hot day. All you think of is my naked body and what it might look like to you. You do not care to know what it felt like to be pursued so vilely.' Bitterly she turned her tear-stained face away from him.

'Nay lass,' Billy cried hotly, knowing what she had said was true.

'It's just the thought that...' he stopped.

'...that someone has looked at me,' she countered. 'It does not make me different... but it makes you different,' she accused. Billy was silent, for he knew it to be true. Wild imaginings of her white and naked body had flashed into his head, arousing base feelings and jealousy to flood his mind. Leah stood up.

'I thought you were my friend!' she said simply and turned away.

'Ah am,' cried Billy desperately, 'ah am. It's just...' he choked on the words, 'ah'm jealous.' But Leah had gone, running down the fell and the words hung unheard on the clear air.

Even the old man noticed Leah's misery and silence in the next few weeks.

'What's to do?' he asked Billy, but Billy shrugged, unwilling to tell his Father of the depths of his own misery and his unspoken rejection of Leah when she had needed him most. Only the letters to Taylor helped resolve Leah's feelings and in them she poured out all her hurt and confusion, writing to him as if he were her dear friend, which he had indeed become. She had invented a sympathetic and loving persona for him, and wrote to him as someone who would understand her deepest thoughts. No letters from him in return had made her reveal her innermost self and she wrote frankly, the letters an emotional catharsis, secure as she felt that all her feelings would remain secret. She had written to her Mother warmly after searching her soul and realising that all she wanted for her Mother was happiness, but at the back of her mind she could not reconcile the thoughts of leaving the fells to return to the dusty little town of Workington.

Summer

The croziers of bracken unfurled on the hillside and the ewes and lambs were returned to the heaf to remain there till July. Summer came in a glorious profusion of greens and golds and pinks enclosed by the blue bowl of the sky. In July, the sheep were washed in the dubs in the deep pools by the becks and it was common for farmers and their men to journey from farm to farm to help with the clipping.

One day in mid-July, the clippers arrived at Cold Harbour Farm. The clipping was done in the old-fashioned way with the long sharp clippers. Each sheerer sitting astride his clipping stool taking the pointed little heads of the sheep under their arm and clipping away at the rug-like fleece with amazing speed. Some shearers could shear as many as seventy or eighty sheep in a day. Leah moved amongst the shearers, carrying ale and bread and cheese. Her skin was golden from the long summer sun and her hair bleached nearly white. She wore it high on the top of her head in a coronet and Billy thought he had never seen anything as beautiful. He could not take his eyes off her. She moved gracefully among the men accepting their banter and their open admiration with good humour, admiring the prowess of the shearer, ever ready with a smile and a word or more refreshment. Billy was proud of her yet eaten by the glances she received, moving ever closer to her but crushed by her icy politeness towards him. Jealousy was an unfamiliar and unwelcome emotion. He had had his pleasures easily before meeting Leah and relinquished them as easily. Since first seeing Leah, he had had no desire for another female body to slake his passions. No deep emotions such as these had ever troubled his mind. As the night wore on and the clipping was over, the ale flowed and the men got rowdier and rowdier. A fiddle was played and voices were raised in country songs in release after the arduous day.

'Yon's a fine maid, Billy,' one of the men chaffed Billy.

'Does she mek thee bed?'

'Aye, tell us, Billy. Does she look after thee at night as well?' ventured another, laughing at Billy's discomfiture. Billy advanced towards them threateningly.

'Tek tha back!' he demanded.

'Sorry, Billy,' the first youth apologised hastily, for Billy's physical prowess was well known, 'only a joke.'

'Aye, only a joke,' agreed the other placatingly, for Billy was very popular and they did not wish to upset him whatever their private conjecture. There were cries of 'Shame!' from the other men and Billy, for the sake of peace turned away with a smile.

Soon the clippers slept where they fell in the barns amongst the fraying hay, content after a good day's work done, with prospect of more days under the sun. Billy went to bed, his head abuzz with ale and the teasing remarks of his friends, a little the worse for wear, his skin warm with the sun, his body aflame for Leah. He walked into the bathroom and ran the cold water over his hands and face, thrusting his dark curls under the flood in an attempt to cool his desire. Groaning he walked softly down the corridor to Leah's room and opened the door. It was almost dawn and the room was illuminated by a rosy glow. Leah lay deeply asleep. She was sleeping like a child on her back with her arms raised behind her head like a defenceless child. She was naked, barely covered by a sheet which clung to the contours of her ripe body. Her pale hair spread out on the pillow and over her full breasts. Billy felt a desire to possess her and to love her, break open in him like a flame and he moved closer to the bed. He looked down at her, at the dark lashes shielding the grey eyes and very slowly and deliberately he pulled down the sheet and looked at her naked body. He looked at her for long moments, physically savouring the sight of her pale nakedness, nearly bursting with desire until a drop of moisture from his wet hair fell upon her rounded stomach, just above the pale triangle open to him. Leah stirred, too deeply tired to awake and Billy was suddenly overcome with shame. He remembered his oath to protect her and never to lay a hand on her and swiftly pulled up the sheet and left the room fearful now lest he wake her. Silently, sober now, he crept down the passage to his own room to lie awake thinking of Leah's defenceless body with a mixture of shame and ecstasy. He remembered his physical reaction to the reason she had left the Hall and shame rose in his throat. He had vowed to protect her and he would do so even if it was from himself. The words 'I love her' slid unbidden into his mind and whispered in his brain and were the last thoughts before he slid into a deep and dreamless sleep.

*

The great circle of the year turned and Billy and his Father were away many days at Tup Fairs when tups were shown and hired out for the season. The Harvest was gathered in, and Billy, his Father and Leah stood in the church to rejoice over the laden produce. Sheaves of corn decorated the pulpit, polished rosy apples lay along the window sills, turnips and carrots and cabbages and leeks and potatoes were piled high in careless profusion. The great urns of the church were filled with shaggy purple marguerites and the altar adorned with bread baked in the shapes of sheaves of wheat or fishes. The golden light of a mellow morning flooded through the stained-glass windows dancing on the abundant produce with burnished light. Leah stood between the old man and Billy, feeling totally and utterly happy, the smell and the light and the warmth of the church, her acceptance by the villagers filled her with peace. She looked surreptitiously first at Billy and then at the old man and the thought came into her head, how I will miss them. The day suddenly grew cold, and the light seemed to fade and the smell of the produce grew overpowering. She looked at Billy and knew that she loved him, that she didn't want to leave him or the farm or the old man. She wanted to stay in the wide fells which stretched as far as the eye could see, to be part of this small community, to belong to Billy. She felt helpless, for Billy had never by word or deed indicated any feelings towards her except friendship and had talked this morning about the Martinmas Fair and hiring a man to do the work the old man was no longer capable of doing. Her heart grew cold. She had served her purpose and now they no longer needed her. Absently, she shook the vicar's outstretched hand, not heeding his pleasant greeting, and silently walked with the old man and Billy back over the golden fells to the farm. Billy too was in torment. All his being cried out to him to take a chance and declare his love to her, he longed for some sign from Leah but none came and he resolved not to make a fool of himself by blurting out his love.

The old man stood in the hallen, at the open front door where Leah had entered a year ago.

'Eh, ah'll miss you, lass,' he said, his old voice breaking, for he too had learned to love Leah and hoped that she might give a sign that she might stay, and yet he too was too proud to ask.

'I'll miss you too Mr Bowman,' said Leah, concentrating all her being not to cry. She stood on tiptoes and kissed his stubbly cheek then turned without a backward glance to where Billy and the trap were waiting.

The journey to Cockermouth took all morning but there was no hurry as Leah was to catch the afternoon train to Workington where her Mother and Mr Beck would meet her. The wedding was to be in a few days. The golden day mocked Leah's thoughts and silence lay heavy between Billy and herself. Soon enough they drove into the crowded main street of Cockermouth, the air filled with merrymaking as it had been the year before. The streets were crowded and Leah said suddenly to Billy, 'Just set me down at the Appletree and I'll make my own way.'

'Ah'll tekk you till the station,' said Billy fiercely, but Leah just as fiercely said she wanted to go on her own. Billy drew the trap to a halt at the Appletree and handed down Leah and her suitcase. They looked at each other for a long moment then Leah put out her hand, 'Thanks Billy,' she said huskily, 'for rescuing me.'

'Thank you Leah for teaching me to read and write,' said Billy. They stood looking at each other helplessly, then the horse grew restless. As Billy turned to gentle it Leah turned away and quickly plunged into the crowd. When Billy looked up she was gone. With a muffled curse he shouted for the stable boy.

'Well, Billy. Are you going to hire any more maids this year?' a voice joked. It was his friend John Bell.

'No. One's enough,' said Billy shortly and despite himself, 'there'll nivver be one the same as her.'

'Then you'd better hire her again,' teased John Bell. Billy looked at him, a great silly grin breaking over his face.

'John,' he shouted, 'John. Thank you,' and turning on his heels leaving the bemused John Bell behind, he plunged into the crowd. He ran frantically, looking for the tall figure, through the amusements and swings and roundabouts he ran, heedless of the glances he received until at last inspiration came to him. Swiftly he ran up Castlegate, and there she was, watching the Hirings.

'Leah!' he shouted, 'Leah!' She spun round on hearing his voice. Her heart leapt like a wild thing and then she was in his arms; she could feel his heart pounding in his chest, smell the warm spicy smell of him. Billy, her Billy. He pushed her away from him and stood looking down at her. His hand strayed upwards and touched her hair. He could see by the look in her grey eyes what she felt and all his heart swelled in happiness, his rough hand stroked her cheek. She stood as if hypnotised, looking, drowning in his green eyes, clear as glass, looking at his handsome face and the curve of his mouth, knowing without a doubt that she was his and he was hers, that they belonged together.

'Leah,' she heard him ask quietly, 'can ah hire thee?' His green eyes twinkled and the white teeth shone against the brown skin and he held her close so close that he could not hear her whisper, 'Yes Billy. For ever.'

Marriage

Leah and Billy were married in the little church in Caldbeck. They married in early December, in the late afternoon of a sharp sunny day. Oil lamps were lit in the gloom of the old church and the atmosphere was warm with expectancy as Leah walked down the church towards Billy, her face bright with happiness and love. The little church was packed, Leah's Mother was there, now Mrs Beck, and Leah had asked her stepfather to give her away. It was a question of who was more proud that day, Billy or Wilson Beck, who now owned a chain of grocery stores throughout west Cumbria and had caused amazement in the village by arriving in a large shiny new motor car. Leah had no idea that Billy had so many friends and relatives or that she herself had been so popular in the village. Billy's Father stood tall and proud by Leah's Mother, a great contentment in his heart at Billy's transparent happiness and joy that his son's deep love had been returned. Billy had only eyes for Leah. He had loved her since the first moment he saw her and that love was stronger and purer with every day that passed. To know that she returned that love had transformed his life and he resolved to care for her and work for her 'Till death us do part' came into his head, part of the solemn vow he was about to make.

Aye. That's it, he thought, till death us do part. He turned his head, and saw his beloved Leah walking towards him. She put out her hand to him, her lovely, handsome, kind and steadfast Billy, and he moved as in a dream towards her to take her hands in his big rough ones. Green eyes met grey then Billy's dazzling smile shone out, his white teeth flashing, his handsome face lit up by his love. Leah caught her breath at the message in those shining eyes, the closeness of the full red mouth and a wave of intense physical desire swept over her, frightening her with its intensity. Turning away from the message in Billy's eyes she tried hard to concentrate on the vicar as he began the time smoothed words which would make them man and wife.

The service over, Billy and Leah walked hand in hand down the aisle. Tears sprang to Hannah Fletcher's eyes as she looked at her daughter's radiant happiness. She had never looked into the future; life in the present had been too tough to speculate about it, but her life, and Leah's had taken an unexpected twist since Taylor O'Neill had inadvertently precipitated Leah's dismissal. She turned to look at Wilson Beck and slipped her hand into his. He held it tenderly, turning to her with a reassuring smile and to offer her his linen handkerchief to dry her tears. Outside the church, the local children had tied up the gates and a cry of 'Shell out, shell out!' went up. Billy, as was the custom, threw a handful of coppers to the children who happily scrabbled in the dust for the pennies and halfpennies. The wedding party walked back over the fells. Wilson Beck had offered the use of his car but Leah and Billy had wanted to walk back over the ancient rough paths to the farm. The day was dying scarlet and gold, the shadows were lengthening over the fells, and the air was sharp with frost and the sounds of their feet on the stones and the happy conversation echoed over the hills. Billy and Leah did not talk much. Billy still held Leah's hand as if he would never let it go but from time to time he turned and looked at her, his green eyes deep with love and a kindling desire to be alone with her and make her his. Leah returned his look with equal intensity. She felt the pull of his sensuality and the depth of his desire. All the time she had lived at Cold Harbour Farm she had never let herself acknowledge her physical attraction to him, and he had given no sign to her in his desire to keep his vow, but now, she felt a shiver through her body, now, tonight, she would be his, his to do as he wished, she would be his woman. Her face burned at the thought and she turned away from him, almost shy at the feelings pulsing through her body. The farm's lights beckoned them in the gloom, there were lights at every window and smoke coming out of every chimney. Home, thought Leah, home. The thought filled her heart with joy and she looked to the old man to smile at him and then to her Mother, walking along so straight and proud behind her.

'We're home,' she said to Billy so softly that no one else could hear. He bent to catch her whisper and his hand came up to touch the white blonde hair he so loved.

'Aye, lass,' he replied, 'our home. And,' he added, 'our children's home.'

Leah looked up at him and smiled a secret smile, her grey eyes telling him all he needed to know.

Wilson Beck had given Leah and Billy a sizeable amount of money as a wedding present. Leah's 'dowry' he lightly called it. Billy and Leah had put some aside, the rest Billy had given to Leah to use as she liked, to buy some clothes for her, he said. She had used some of it for herself but most of it to make the farm more comfortable, for new curtains and cushions and bed linen and crockery and the softening touches a woman could bring to the somewhat spartan house. Inside the great room, the fire glowed and splashed sparkles of light on the old polished copper and pewter, thick curtains hung over the window to keep out the draught and bright cushions softened the old wooden chairs and settle. A smell of tatie pot filled with meat and black pudding wafted appetisingly from the polished range. After a warming drink, the party, with much laughter went into the barn next to the farm. The floor had been cleared and swept, bales of sweet smelling hay were pulled up the length of the building. The walls had been whitewashed and many oil lamps placed in the niches. A shallow platform had been erected for the musicians and a long table held the steaming tatie pot and platters of ham, cheese, new bread, the pale farm butter, big slabs of cake and large pottery jugs of strong ale. Leah had hired girls from the village to serve the food and they carefully carried round the steaming tatie pot to guests who suddenly found themselves ravenously hungry, tempted by the delicious smell. After eating, the real business of dancing and drinking began. The barn echoed to the squeak and wail of the music, the lights spun shadows on the walls and flickered up to the rafters, the dancers spun and twirled in the heat and warmth and happiness. Outside a cold hard moon shone down and frost began to silver the barren trees and fells, the tarn slowly hardened over and a thin wind slid round the old farm. But the old walls were solid and the dancers too flushed with food and dancing to care. Billy and Leah danced only with each other, their eyes only on each other, the pull of their bodies attracting like magnets until at the height of the dancing Billy pulled Leah into the shadows and kissed her, his warm beer smelling mouth enveloping her. The shadows swirled crazily and she gave herself up to him, pressing her body against his to feel the whole warm male length of him. She trembled against him, her whole body roused at his kiss. Billy trembled too, holding her close, the warm smell of her young aroused skin in his nostrils. He pushed her away from him gently and putting his arm round her said huskily, 'Come lass.' They left the dancers and the noise and the music without a backward glance, caring nought for their guests, and any who saw their rapt and dream-like faces smiled in understanding and a little jealousy. Billy drew Leah into the empty house and up the stairs silent as sleep walkers, the slow tick of the grandfather clock standing in the hallway seemed to echo the slow drum of their heartbeats. They were to sleep in Billy's room and Billy drew her gently through the door. A fire had been lit in the small iron fireplace and the room was warm, and soft shadows flickered and danced on the walls mirroring the patterns of the old latticed fireguard with the brass rail. The curtains were open and moonlight streamed into the room through the old glass. Billy kissed Leah again with a hungry intensity which started her trembling anew.

'Take your clothes off for me lass,' he demanded softly, 'I want to look at you.'

Leah looked at Billy, startled and afraid, then seeing the look in his eyes, gleaming in the moonlight, her desire for him overcame her modesty. Slowly, she unbuttoned her dress and dropped it to the floor. She heard the sharp intake of Billy's breath and a feeling of her power over him and a longing to seduce him overcame her. With infinite care and a desire to show her body to him she made her movements more languid and subtle, her pulses thudding as she slowly took off her clothes until they lay crumpled at her feet. Billy watched her in the moonlight, his heart beating like thunder in his ears whilst all the time she held him with her gaze, her grey eyes silver in the moonlight, the shadows from the firelight caressing her body. He watched her until at last she stood before him unashamed in her nakedness, and he let his eyes slowly, slowly wander over her tall and slender body. He had only guessed at her beauty in his wildest dreams but the sight of her, lovely and unafraid, waiting for him to possess her, stunned his senses. His eyes caressed the full thrusting breasts and the slim waist, down the childishly rounded stomach to the pale triangle between her long well-shaped legs.

'Do you like me, Billy?'

Leah's question breathed into the silence.

'Aye, lass. Ah like you,' he replied, moving to her to pull out the combs in her hair, hair he had longed to touch since the first time he met her. It slid soft as silk over his trembling hands and down her body to part cover her naked flesh. He gathered a handful and pressed its sweet smelling softness to his lips, liquid silver in the moonlight. Leah pushed him away and very deliberately put up her trembling hands and shrugged his jacket off his shoulders.

Leah undressed Billy slowly and lovingly with no shame. His buttons yielding to her fingers, she smoothed the linen shirt from his shoulders and drew it away from his warm skin. The smell of him reminded her of her first night at Cold Harbour, lying in his bed, afraid of the future and she smiled a small secret smile as carefully as if in an erotic dream she traced the smooth skin of his shoulders letting her fingertips linger on his nipples touching them sweetly and gently. He shivered under her touch, standing in a trance of desire. She pulled him close to her so that her full breasts melted into his warm skin, her slender arms reached up to pull down his handsome face and she kissed him slowly and sweetly before bending low before him, her hair covering her nakedness as she gently pulled down the woollen trousers over his slim hips. Her hands felt the beautiful line of his body and kneeling at his feet, her hair a covering cloak, she unlaced his shoes and drew off his stockings. He stood before her, trembling and almost afraid of the feeling she had aroused in him. Her fingers caressed his aroused flesh gently and carefully as if she were blind, and she slowly stood up to trace again the shape of his body and felt the warmth of him quivering to her touch. She took his hands and cupped them round her breasts, the full nipples pushing against his fingers then moved away deliberately to look at him. They stood naked for long minutes and looked at each other, the moonlight silvering their bodies, the leaping shadows of the fire making them look like two mythical ethereal creatures. Billy was beautiful, his tall body was well muscled and strong. His broad shoulders tapered away to a slim waist and slim hips, Leah's eyes lingered on the dark bush of his hair and his manhood, firm and erect. His legs were surprisingly well shaped with long narrow feet, his handsome face was unsmiling and intent.

'Do you like me, lass?' he asked, imitating Leah's question.

'Aye, lad. Ah like you,' she sighed in answer. Billy took her hand and pulled her to the bed, his desire for her making him forget that she might be afraid at his ardour but Leah was not afraid, their lovemaking was as natural as breathing and she gave herself to him with no reservations, caught up in the moonlight and the flickering shadows of the fire, the maleness of him and his beautiful body. Billy's leaping passion mingled with love and desire overwhelmed them both and he came in great shuddering gasps, feeling her moist and warm responding to him in an arch of release.

'Leah. Leah,' he called, his great cry echoing through the silent house. 'Leah. Ah love you. Ah love you.' Leah, arching against his body, her whole being spilling from her in a sweetness she could never have imagined cried out to answer.

'Billy. Billy, I love you.'

Still the dancers danced in the warm and noisy barn whilst Billy and Leah made love to touch the stars in the warm room with only the cold and watching moon sliding through the mottled glass to see their ecstasy.

War

The next three years flew by for Billy and Leah. As the circle of the years turned in a golden span, so they learned to love each other more. The farm prospered and expanded as Billy, in his great happiness, worked hard for Leah and the children they both longed for. Each day began and ended with Leah at his side and he was content to look into a future where they grew old together and their sons, for he was sure they would be sons, would take his place. And if children never arrived, well, what did it matter. Leah was all he wanted and would ever need. Billy loved Leah as his soul mate and cherished their shared life like a precious jewel. Many times as he walked back to the farm after a day on the high fells he thanked his God for the wonderful gift of Leah's love. Leah in her turn blossomed under the shelter and strength of Billy's love and consistency, finding in him a depth of passion and feeling which never ceased to amaze her. They still learned together and read together, using Taylor O'Neill's money to furnish their ever growing collection of books, and although their world was small, their minds were open. They could see their world was changing and that even their little corner of the universe would be touched by the outside events of a restless world. Leah still wrote to Taylor O'Neill far away in America and if Billy was a little jealous he was wise enough to keep silent. Leah had told him of the conversations which had first opened her mind. She had grown used to writing to

Taylor and expected no reply. In fact, the very lack of reply had made her write to him as a dear friend, openly and movingly, chronicling her ever growing love for Billy and the simple lives they led on the farm on the Cumbrian fells. She wrote of the books they read and discussed and the widening interests they shared. The Liverpool shipping agent's office had been sold and the new owner consigned the ever growing pile of letters addressed to a stranger in America to a large box in a dusty basement until an industrious clerk intrigued by the growing pile of correspondence had eventually dispatched them to Taylor's shipping office in Boston. For Taylor O'Neill now was a well-known name in shipping circles and there they remained as Taylor continued in his restless travels and in making his fortune.

One hot day in August 1914 changed Billy and Leah's lives, as well as those of millions of others' for ever. War was declared with Germany and its evil fingers touched even the remote villages of Cumberland. In 1914, Field Marshal Lord Kitchener, hero of the Sudanese and Boer War, called for one hundred thousand young men to join the Army as volunteers for three years. The British Expeditionary Force was forced to retreat at Mons and the intimidating poster with its accusatory finger took on a new meaning and within the first three weeks one hundred thousand volunteers joined the Army. By September, the number had swelled to five hundred thousand. Kitchener had promised that groups of friends from the same village or town could fight together and 'Pals Battalions' were formed inside the new army which reflected the origin of the men. In far away and isolated Cumberland, Lord Lonsdale decided to recruit a battalion of his own to fight against his former friend the Kaiser who had stayed many times at Lowther Castle for the shooting season. Lonsdale's recruiting posters were in every village and town of Cumberland. Leah, her heart filled with dread, stared white-faced at the poster in the village shop in Caldbeck. The recruiting poster was in red, yellow and white, the racing colours of the Earl and the slogan 'Are you a mouse or a man?' shrieked its message to her fearful eyes. The shopkeeper looked at Leah's pale face.

'Eh, Leah lass,' she said kindly, 'your Billy won't have to go. Who'd look after the farm?'

But the words did not comfort Leah whose blood seemed to chill in her veins at the thought of Billy, her gentle Billy, having to fight in some foreign country for she knew not what. On the long walk home from the village, over the well-walked path which she had walked as Billy's bride, she looked round her as with new eyes. How beautiful it was. The colours of high summer flared around her and the clear blue dome of the sky soared above her, but her spirit felt strangely cold. She shuddered superstitiously as the sun over the Solway was reflected in a deep path of gold and crimson and scarlet spilling into the sea. Like blood, she thought, like blood. She stood for a moment as a blade of animal-like fear shot through her body and her eyes dammed with tears. That night, she clung to Billy's beautiful body as if she would never let him go.

'Billy, Billy,' she pleaded, 'swear to me that you'll not join up. You don't have to go. Let someone else go. Swear to me Billy.'

There was silence in the darkness then Billy's voice came, rough in stoic resignation, 'Ah can't swear to you, lass. Ah can't. Not even for you. Ah, can't swear.'

'Oh, Billy,' Leah called out in anguish and pulled his head down to hers in love and pity as she found his lips. Tears cascaded down her face and to her surprise she felt

Billy's tears mingle with hers as he held her as if he would never let her go.

It was only a week later that Billy made his decision. He was home later than usual, and Leah, with a sixth sense, waited restlessly for his homecoming. She did not go to meet him on the fells as she would ordinarily have done, but waited in the warm and bright room as if its familiar loveliness would bring her comfort. The old man caught her anxiety and looked frequently at her white and strained face. He did not offer words of comfort for he knew only too well the rush of blood and the fever that impelled men to join the colours, for he himself had fought for Queen and country when only a lad. Leah and the old man waited silently as Billy's feet clattered in the kitchen, waited as he washed his hands and both turned in one accord to look at him as he entered the room. Billy looked at them, the two beings he loved with all his heart, his green eyes bright with unshed tears.

'You've done it Billy, haven't you?' Leah called out in a high strange voice. Billy nodded, the tears sliding unchecked down his cheeks. He moved to take Leah into his arms but she turned away with a cry of anguish and the old man moved towards him.

'Billy,' he said gruffly, 'ah'm proud of you, lad. You did the right thing.'

He put out his arms and Billy and Leah drew close to him, feeling like children in his strong clasp.

That night Billy made love to Leah as if it were the first time. He held her long slim body to him as if he would never let her go and loved her with his mind and body and soul as completely as one human being can love another. Afterwards, in the silence when they lay close together, he stroked her hair gently until she slept, then lay, dry-eyed in the darkness, feeling more lonely than he had ever felt in his life. Along the corridor the old man too lay awake. He knew what fearful experiences his son would have to go through, his gentle Billy, and he turned his faded green eyes to the rough wall and prayed for Billy as tears forced their way down his worn and wrinkled cheeks.

Camp

The Lonsdales camped on the racecourse at Blackwell in Carlisle which became the Battalion Headquarters on September 25th, 1914. The command of the Lonsdales was taken over by Colonel Percy Wilfred Machell CMG of Crackenthorpe Hall. Lord Lonsdale had asked him to come out of retirement and train and command the Lonsdales. The Colonel was fifty-two years old and had many years experience as a regular soldier. He became the heart and soul of the battalion and welded together inexperienced farmhands, servants, miners, iron and steel workers, clerks and office workers, into soldiers. Although Carlisle was only thirty miles away from Caldbeck, it might have been on the moon and Leah and Billy's Father relied on the regular letters sent by Billy for their news. The pain of Billy's departure was with Leah every waking moment and even in her dreams. Many of Caldbeck's young men had joined the colours too and every small village and town in Cumberland had lost its sons and Fathers, sweethearts and husbands, to the recruiting officers and the camp at Blackwell had the pick of Cumberland and Westmoreland's youth training and drilling in high spirits, some of them so young that their only fear was that the war would be over before they could fight. Billy wrote to Leah as much as he could and as often as he could. In November he wrote,

My dearest girl,

The weather has taken a turn for the worse. How wet and cold it is. I can see the Caldbeck Fells from the camp, their tops covered in mist. I imagine you at home, before the fire. I wish I were beside you reading, looking up to see your beautiful face, the firelight shining on your hair. I see the old man sitting opposite with Holly at his feet. How I wish I were with you. Richardsons (the builders from Penrith) cannot work to build the hutments, the weather is so bad and the camp is a sea of cold mud. Lord Lonsdale has sent us a thousand great coats and blankets from London and we have been issued with a uniform in the Hodden. The grey wool reminds me of the Herdwicks. Is the lad I hired working all right? You must tell me if he's not, although I know it's quiet at this time of year. Lord Lonsdale has issued us all with a silver cap badge. He designed it himself, it's got a dragon on it, although someone told me it's a griffin (but I don't know what the difference is), with the name of the battalion under it. Something to give our sons when they arrive, and I'm sure they will one day, dearest Leah. Tell the old man I love him, for I can never say it to his face.

Your loving husband Billy

From January to March the training kept on relentlessly turning the disparate group of men into a fighting force. Men were selected to train as scouts, signallers, machine gunners, stretcher bearers, all of them selected to play some role in the mechanics of War. They practised attacks and dug trenches and trained hard, learning to obey orders and to rely on each other in a spirit of friendliness and good humour. In April, Billy came home on leave. It was a warm spring and a faint sheen of green was covering the larches on the fells, a skylark spiralled its song into the clear blue air as Billy walked up the well-worn paths over the fells to the farm. Billy had not told Leah of his leave, wanting to surprise her and as he walked, he anticipated holding her in his arms again and seeing her grey eyes light up and the special intimate smile she had only for him. Leah was walking down the fell to Caldbeck to do some shopping when she saw his familiar figure. For a moment, Leah thought that she was dreaming and that her desire for Billy had produced him in her imagination, and then her heart leapt as she recognised his tall figure.

'Billy. Billy!' she called, her cry reaching him in the clear air.

'Leah!' he threw down his heavy pack and ran towards her, stumbling in his eagerness to be near her, to be close to her, to be with her again. They held each other as if they would never let each other go. At last he drew away from her. She was thinner than when he had left her and her face had matured from that of a young girl into a woman, her face marked by loss and longing, but the grey eyes dazzled him and unbidden, unthinking, his hand reached out to touch her hair and pull out the pins that bound it.

'Oh, Billy,' she blushed in confusion as her hair, sparkling in the sunlight, fell over her shoulders. Unsmiling, Billy stood and watched her, his green eyes dark with desire and longing. Recognising the look in Billy's eyes, feeling strong desire sweep through her, Leah took Billy's arm and led him off the path, through the spring bracken round an outcrop of the fell where they would be unseen from the path. Gently Billy took off his hodden great coat and laid it in the grass in the shelter of the rock and very carefully, as if in a dream he laid Leah down and stretched himself beside her.

'Oh Billy. Your hair,' Leah called out in her anguish, for Billy's unruly black curls had gone and in their place was a short dark stubble. She studied his face carefully. The laughing boy, her darling Billy had vanished and in his place was a man, a soldier. She shivered slightly, then Billy smiled his familiar lazy smile and she relaxed into his arms, her face against the grey hard wool of his uniform. They told each other of their love and longing for each other and it was there under the arching sky, bodies, lips and souls entwined, that Billy and Leah's child was conceived.

France

At the beginning of May 1915, the Lonsdales left the camp at Blackwell to begin their final training in preparation for France. The streets of Carlisle were packed as they marched towards the Citadel Station, Saint Stephen's Military Band leading the battalion. One thousand three hundred and fifty men had joined the Lonsdales. Lord Lonsdale inspected the battalion which was led by Colonel Machell. Leah, the old man, Leah's Mother and Wilson Beck stood amongst the cheering and flag waving crowds, caught up despite themselves in the excitement, stirred by the music and the pride in the cream of Cumberland's youth marching to war. Leah had kept her head bare so that Billy might easier see her in the throng and Captain James Forbes Robertson, marching with his men, caught a glimpse of the flaxen hair as he marched resolutely along. Memories of earlier far-off innocent times flooded into his mind and he walked along unseeing with a bitter longing for happier times rising up in his breast and threatening to bring tears into his eyes. James too had been overcome with patriotic fervour and had joined the Lonsdales. His school days long over, he had fulfilled his ambition of travelling until at last, on the death of his Father the Captain, he had returned to Netherghyll Hall to look after the estates and care for his ageing Mother and as yet unmarried sister. In his knapsack was hidden a sketchbook and pencils, for his boyhood passion still remained and gave him pleasure. He turned to catch again the glimpse of white blonde hair. Yes, he was almost sure that it was Leah. How strange that on this of all days he should see her. He shrugged and walked on, no doubt she would be married with a brood of children, he thought cynically. Billy too was searching for a glimpse of Leah's silken hair. His green eyes were clouded with tears for it broke his heart to be parted from Leah. At last he saw her and instinctively broke ranks to sweep her in his arms and kiss her with a passion which raised a roar from the watching crowds. The sergeant bawled at him and with a desperate smile to Leah he ran to join his friends, beginning his long journey to the War.

*

November 1915

My dearest Leah,

At last the long training is over and on the 15th we cross the channel for Boulogne. Our troopship is called 'Princess Victoria.' The sooner we go there the sooner this war is over and I can return to you and our child. I think of the child often, fast in its secret sea, moving and growing, waiting for the time to join us. What a wonderful child he or she will be, a new start in a crazy world. Oh, how I wish I were with you in our farm, in the warm bright home you have made for us. How wrong it feels to be going to fight other men. I have always saved the lives of animals and cared for them, it seems so wicked to think of fighting and yet that is what I have been trained for, and Leah, if killing some other man means I get home quicker to you my darling and to the old man then I swear I will do it...

In the middle of December, the battalion arrived on the western front near the town of Albert, a place where nearly all the troops marched through on their way to the front line. Billy gazed, horrified at the muddy chalky paths which led through a network of trenches. The paths slowly sank until the surface of the ground was above his head and over all the desolation wafted a sweet sickly smell which all too soon he was to recognise as the smell of death mingled with sweat and lime and excrement. Horrified, he saw that the dugouts were only holes scraped into the mud, in many places there were no duckboards and the mud and water was four or five foot deep. The horror of the trenches was intensified when the Lonsdales took their turn in the line to give them experience in trench warfare. Nothing in Billy's wildest imaginings could have equalled the despair of being in the front line. Billy learned to live with the thought of imminent and sudden death although the cacophony of exploding shells tore at his nerves and the whine of the snipers' bullets flayed his raw imagination. He saw his first death, no one he knew personally, just a young man, alive one instant and the next his chest torn open by a snipers bullet, fall, hands outstretched into the grasping mud, his thick scarlet blood gushing to mingle with the putrid, the ever-present water. Billy turned his head away and cried, his throat retched in a spasm of fear.

'Leah. Oh Leah,' he whispered, trying to conjure up a vision of her face to shield him from the stark inevitability of death.

*

The old man died in December. Since Billy's departure he had literally faded away. Even the joy of the soon-to-be-born baby which had cheered his spirits for a while could not assuage the longing he had for his only son. His dark imaginings and his knowledge of war as it was in all its horror, without any false heroics, sapped his spirit. For after all, Billy and he had never been parted since Billy's birth, except for the odd day or two, and he felt Billy's absence with an intensity of pain which was unremitting. One night, as they sat by the fire, as they had done so many times with Billy, he took Leah's hands in his own old and weathered ones.

'If ought happens to Billy, lass,' he said falteringly, 'you know the farm and all there is is yours?'

Leah shuddered superstitiously.

'Don't talk like that, Dad,' she replied painfully, 'Billy will be back soon and we'll all be as we were.'

Deep in her heart however, she knew that nothing could be the same, for Billy's letters were increasingly bleak with an undertone of despair easy to decipher by his loved ones.

'Ah'm tired, lass,' the old man murmured, 'and ah miss our Billy,' he ended pitifully.

'Oh Dad, so do I,' moaned Leah, and she put her arms round the now frail shoulders and took him in her arms as she had done Billy and rocked him and cried with him in sorrow for him, and Billy so far away.

One winter's night, with an unrelenting moon hard in the sky, the wind moaned sneakily round the old house, twisting in at the old green glass windows, scurrying down the passages. Leah had lit fires in the bedrooms but it seemed as if nothing could keep out the chill wind. The old man dozed fitfully by the fire and Leah looked at him with pity. He seemed so old and frail. The child within her moved urgently and she placed her hand on her swelling stomach to gain comfort from Billy's child moving within her. The tick of the grandfather clock seemed to boom in her ears and she dropped her book to stare into the fire and move the glowing coals with the poker in an attempt to warm her heart. Suddenly the old man stood up, casting off the blankets which had warmed his old body. He straightened and it was as if Leah could see him as she had seen him when she came to the farm all those years ago.

How like Billy he was. His green eyes glowed and he took a pace towards the centre of the room.

'Billy,' he called, his voice thick and strong, 'our Billy. I'm coming!'

Leah froze in fright. The conviction in the old man's voice almost made her believe that Billy would walk in through the door.

'Billy!' the old man called again, 'Our Billy!' He stumbled and then very slowly crumpled to the floor. Leah knew without knowing how that the old man was dead.

They buried the old man in Caldbeck churchyard beside the beautiful old church where he had worshipped his God so simply. The churchyard was full of mourners for death seemed to touch them all with a universally uniting finger. Already the small villages and towns of Cumberland were making their personal sacrifices to the unrelenting war. Leah acknowledged sympathies as in a dream, the imminent birth of her and Billy's child somehow insulating her from thoughts of the future. The old man's lawyers had visited her; Billy and she now owned the farm. The old man had been thrifty, for after all what had he to spend his money on? Billy had made provision for her before his departure too. Leah walked back over the fells, alone in the fading winter's afternoon. Her Mother and Wilson Beck had wanted to accompany her but Leah had insisted tiredly that she needed to be on her own, and at last after many protestations they had given in to her wishes. The farm seemed to huddle down in the bleak landscape and the sombre greys and blacks of the shadowed fells seemed to echo Leah's sorrow. Billy's uncle, the old man's brother from nearby Uldale was to farm the farm for her.

'Till our Billy comes back, lass,' he said to her gently, his dark eyes warm with sympathy for her and the unborn child.

'Ah'll cope wid it all, Leah. You just stay well for the bairn.' She had hired a young girl to help in the house and the oil lamps were lit in the windows as was the custom but Leah drew no comfort from the lights and sat that night gazing into the fire. The lovely room seemed to wrap itself round her but she missed the old man's presence and the comfort of him sitting opposite her and their talk of Billy. Where was Billy now? In what foreign hell, away from her and the child soon to be born. How soon happiness turned to sorrow, how short her time had been in this old building compared to that of the old man. She resolved not to write to Billy and tell him of the death of his Father. It would be too cruel when he was in the midst of death. Time enough when he returned to share their grief. She wrapped her arms round her unborn child and stared unseeing into the fire until the embers sighed and sank and died, then slowly like an old woman she dragged herself up the stairs in the cold house with only the heartbeat of the clock and the moan of a sneaky wind to break the silence.

Billy and Leah's child was born on the last night of the old year. The villages and towns of Cumberland had little to celebrate or to look forward to in the new year for they were decimated by the deaths of their young men and many a home that night was full of grief and sorrow for a new year which held no child or lover or Father. William Michael Bowman, or Will as he was to be called ever after, made his way easily and quickly into the world, causing as little fuss as he would all his life. He lay in Leah's arms looking at her intently as she put him to her breast, her heart spilling over with love for her son. His big dark eyes, later as green as his Father's, seemed to reassure her of a future and a continuity in her life. She held him close to her, feeling the little eager mouth pull at her ready nipple with a sweet painful tug. She looked down at the shock of black hair and softly spoke to him of his Father who would love him as she would. She closed her eyes and thought of Billy and suddenly he seemed very close to her. She could imagine him standing close to her, stroking the downy head of the new born child and she smiled as she imagined Billy counting the boy's toes and fingers and planning the time he would grow up and be a companion to him on the farm. The lamplight flickered and the shadows of the firelight leaped and danced on the old walls and she felt Billy there in an almost mystical union as surely as if he had spoken to her. She dare not open her eyes the feeling was so strong. In the trenches far away Billy felt the telepathic pull of Leah's joy in the birth of their son and he found himself smiling for the first time for months so sure was he that the child had been born and that all was well. He felt so close to Leah that he felt he could reach out and touch her. Then the child stirred in Leah's arms and the spell was broken.

Death

Billy half leaned, half lay against the trunk of the tree, blankly watching the fingers of a new dawn push away the darkness of the night with a lovely promise of a clear warm day. Billy watched the light intently, the clear translucent greens and blues reminding him of his journey across the Caldbeck Fells when he had first taken Leah to Cold Harbour Farm. His hand strayed without volition to the pocket of his filthy uniform where a long lock of Leah's bright hair lay like a talisman close to his heart. In his pocketbook was a photograph of Leah with the child he had never held in his loving arms. Memories of her flooded into his exhausted brain and he could see her face close, so close to him.

Leah would not have recognised this gaunt soldier as her gorgeous, handsome Billy. The glossy black curls were gone and the brutal crop lay flat and lifeless against his head. The dancing green eyes were dull and haunted by the sights he had seen, their clear green sparkle extinguished. His smooth russet skin was pallid. Billy was so tired, his love of life and his joyous spirit replaced by a dulled comprehension of the cruelty around him which he seemed to have endured for ever. Only the thought of home and Leah had held his sanity together, he had witnessed cruelty and bravery of a staggering kind and he prayed each night that he might face the next test with bravery and dignity, even if it meant killing his fellow men or dying himself. He desperately wanted to live for Leah and to hold his son in his arms; he would never, he swore to himself, let them out of his sight if he could survive the carnage.

The Chantilly Conference in December 1915 had agreed on the overall strategy for 1916 and the unstoppable machinery of war still rumbled on. The French were exhaustedly trying to stem the brutal German offensive at Verdun and desperately needed the British Force to bear the unendurable pressure. Today, Saturday 1st July, one hundred thousand men were waiting to begin the offensive. The Lonsdales too were to take part in the 'Big Push'. The British now had a major role in the offensive, with sixteen divisions to the French five divisions.

For two whole weeks, the guns had thundered and pounded at the German trenches until the very ground trembled. Men, pulverised by the unrelenting, unremitting, heart-stopping thunder, pressed their faces and bodies screaming into the ground, overcome with horror and despair. The hope was that the bombardment would demoralise and disorient the Germans with its ceaseless pounding. Day and night the guns spewed death and destruction, the noise had even been heard across the English Channel. It was rumoured that fifteen hundred shells had fallen on the enemy.

Now on this beautiful morning the movement from the rear to the jumping off trenches was complete and over one hundred thousand men were waiting to do battle. In the overcrowded, foetid trenches men could neither rest nor sleep, and they stood together, enduring the moment with their own individual courage. As the warm and peaceful light flooded the battlefield, men prayed, wondering whether this would be their last day on earth or whether they would be lucky enough to survive the slaughter. The remaining minutes seemed like an eternity on this beautiful day. For a few eerie minutes the artillery stopped fighting and the thunder of Billy's heart pounding in his ears seemed like the beating of the one hundred thousand men. At 7.30 a.m. precisely, the British barrage moved on to the Germans' second line. The whistles blew and men wished each other good luck, some of them clasping hands. Clumsily, they climbed the ladders out of the trenches into the bright morning where death lay waiting.

The Lonsdales were posted in Authille Woods and were to brave the German crossfire to gain the first jumping off trench where the Scottish Highlanders were currently waiting for the signal for attack. James Forbes Robertson was also at Authille Woods. To disguise his fear he was occupying himself by drawing the scenes around him in his ever-present sketchbook. The night before last he had spent in Albert, pushing his seed into a willing girl in desperate affirmation of being alive. It was a wild and passionate coupling.

He had met Mary Flanagan, a dark-eyed Irish nurse, when he had gone to visit some of his men in the staging station at Albert before they were sent back home too wounded to be of any use as cannon fodder. The attraction between him and Mary had been instant and he had spent all his spare time with her. Mary's courage and kindness had almost penetrated the hard shell he had formed round himself to protect him from thinking and feeling about this ghastly War and the terrible destruction around him. Mary had taken him back to her quarters when at last, almost on the eve of battle, their feelings for each other and the thought that they might never meet again had overcome their natural caution and they had clung to each other in pity and passion as the guns pounded in time with their heartbeats. James kissed her goodbye and they looked at each other silent and afraid. He had given her a letter for her to post to his Mother and sister which he had felt in his heart might be his last few scrawled words to them. Last night on return to the lines, James had spoken to Colonel Machell the beloved commander of the Lonsdales. The Colonel was pale and weary.

'I fear all will not go well James,' he had confided. 'If I see that it goes badly I shall come and see it through.'

James was silent. If the Colonel had no hope what hope for the Lonsdales? James looked up at the blue clean morning. He did not want to die but at least he had no loved ones waiting at home for him, dependent on his survival. He thought of Mary and his face grew soft, yet he knew that he had not been the first man in Mary's life and neither would he be the last for the lust for life and the affirmation of passion and feeling was strong in those who were faced with mortal danger. He drew quickly, capturing the faces round him, faces of men sentenced to a dreadful, useless death. How brave they are, he thought with a rush of pride, how brave and how hopeless.

The Highlanders attacked at seven thirty. Half an hour later the Lonsdales moved out of Authille. Clumsily laden by the accoutrements of war, they could not change and so walked to their fate. Billy, as if in the grip of a terrible nightmare, formed up in line with his pals, his rifle across his chest, bayonet at the ready, with the lock of Leah's hair clasped in his sweating hand as if he were holding a magic talisman. Slowly, oh so slowly, they began walking towards the German lines. The Germans had crawled into the fresh air, their uniforms torn and stinking, splattered with the blood of their dead comrades. The air was shaking with the deadly blossom of machine-gun and rifle fire. Billy walked slowly, his head held high. Beside him in the grass, men were scythed down like corn waving in the breeze of the summer morning. They screamed as they lay wounded and dying by his feet, but Billy walked on slowly over the grass, his numbed mind not accepting the reality of the slaughter around him. The Lonsdales were ripped systematically to pieces as the German machine-gunners found their deadly range. Colonel Machell, aghast at the awful slaughter, desperately pushed his way from the rear to lead the men whom he was so proud of, his only thought to be with them whatever the outcome. He staggered to the top of a trench parapet, shouting to urge his men on, but his devotion was rewarded by a mortal wound in his head. His adjutant, a Lieutenant Gordon, who had despairingly stooped over Machell's body to see if he could help him, lay severely wounded. James saw that Major Diggle, the second in command, also lay wounded. Within a few seconds, the battalion was leaderless. James, adrenaline pumping through his body, shouted and urged on his men and they continued their slow advance, but to no avail, catching up with Billy's comrades, or what was left of them, in their hopeless march to annihilation from the German guns. Billy felt no fear now, he was far away, his poor gentle mind had snapped with the horror of it all and as he walked towards his death he was sure he walked on the sunlit Caldbeck Fells. His mind grasped at the thought of Leah, his Leah. And there she was, moving lightly towards him, her hair unbound coming towards him, her arms outstretched, the gentle smile lighting up her face. Billy's green eyes shone and his face lit up with boyish happiness.

'Leah! Leah!' he shouted. The bullet tore into his throat and the words he shouted turned into an unearthly scream and yet still he walked on until, at last he fell, his knees gently buckling and all that was best of Billy Bowman, all his love and his kindness and his gentleness and his joyful lust for life, spilled out on to the torn and weary ground as his blood gently drained away in the grass and his life ebbed to a close. His hand opened on the lock of Leah's bright hair which he had loved so much and his beautiful green eyes stared blankly and unseeingly at the horror all around him. James heard the ghastly shriek of Billy's dying breath and turned to see him fall, as in slow motion, on to the bloody grass. He recognised Billy as the handsome boy, somehow always apart from his fellows, sometimes reading or writing letters, which was unusual for one of his rank. He had drawn him often, surreptitiously, his interest kindled and his artist's eye attracted by Billy's handsome face and his gentle manner to his fellow men as he had drawn many others in their day-to-day life. In the early days, he had drawn Billy throwing back his head and laughing his joyous laugh at some remark and the deft lines had caught Billy's spirit. Impulsively, he moved towards him, although knowing in his heart that there was nothing he could do and was feet away from Billy's outflung hand when the bullet caught him in the shoulder and spun him full circle for another bullet to lodge in his leg and another in his arm causing him to fall to the ground fainting with the pain. Slowly the attack faded away and the dead lay in great swathes before the German lines. Those who survived crouched torn and bloodied, half mad and shocked in the shell holes praying for the day to be over and flinching at the shells which fell like a deadly rain all that blazing hot day. Men tried to help their wounded comrades with water taken from the bodies of the dead and the air echoed with the gunfire and the terrible cries of the wounded and dying and the swarms of flies buzzed and gorged on the running blood. James drifted in and out of consciousness. The blazing sun burned his face and with a mighty effort he turned on to his stomach screaming with the pain which tore his body, his wounded arm outstretched. He lay dazed, trying to absorb the waves of pain which swept through him and his fingers clenching with agony closed round something soft. He opened his eyes to see clasped in his hand a lock of pale white hair bound in a clasp of gold. Billy lay near him, the flies already buzzing round his body and on the drying blood in the ghastly wound, his handsome face unmarked, his green eyes still bright seemed to stare at James in mute surprise. James pushed his face into the grass and cried hard gulping sobs until the pain in his body tore into his senses and he cried for Billy whose staring eyes seemed to epitomise the futility of this dreadful day. At last the day darkened and the unrelenting sun faded from the sky. Those who survived the slaughter began to crawl and stumble back across the bloody battlefield to their own lines. The stretcher bearers, risking their lives as they had done all day, came out to begin the long and horrible task of moving the wounded and the dead, whilst all the time doctors and padres attended to the dying and wounded. The front trench was full of dead and dying men in a great flood of damaged humanity. James and Billy were carried to the trench together and James lay beside Billy's body until someone could carry him to the first aid station. All the while James held on to the lock of hair, the colour and softness of it somehow a symbol of hope to him. When the stretcher bearer finally came for him, James somehow did not want to leave Billy on his own. The stretcher bearer who was barely unable to control his grief at the horror of the sights he had seen was gentle with James and assured him that all would be well with Billy's body.

'I need to know his name,' James insisted weakly, 'we lay together...' he stopped and started to cry, 'we lay like two friends together... the least I can do is pray for him and know his name.' He clung to the arm of the stretcher bearer, 'I need to know his name,' he begged. The stretcher bearer overcome with pity searched Billy's body for identification.

'Please,' protested James weakly, tears coming to his eyes 'please.'

Somehow it seemed terribly important that he should know the name of the man he had laid beside all day long on the hellish battlefield. The bearer fumbled in Billy's blood-drenched pocket and pulled out a small pocketbook.

'Here, his name will be in here.'

He gently put the pocketbook into James's hand. James held on to the book and to the lock of Leah's hair as the night sky whirled and spun and merciful darkness blotted out his pain. On that black day, twenty thousand died for 'King and country' and Leah would never again look on the handsome face of 'her Billy' and see his green eyes light up with love for her and the child he had never seen.

Aftermath

Leah was at the sink when she saw the postman walk into the yard. He carried in his hand a small brown envelope, carried it reverently, his weather-beaten country face closed against emotion. He knew that whatever news it contained it could only be bad. He felt, he confided to his wife in a fit of fancy, like 'The Angel of Death'. All over Cumberland, in every small town and village, blinds were drawn and windows shuttered. The 'Pals' battalions were soon to be disbanded as they gave too much indication of the continuing carnage. How could the news be 'good' people asked themselves when so many of their young men were dying? Leah dried her hands slowly and carefully as if this action would fend off reality. She moved like a sleepwalker through the open door to take the envelope, heedless of the man's muttered remark and walked back into the house carrying the envelope as if it were some rare and precious gift. With exaggerated care she went through into the living room and carefully propped it up on top of the sandstone mantel, then she sat down in one of the wooden chairs and looked at it. The sound of her heart filled her ears in the silence, echoed by the tick of the grandfather clock in the hall. Upstairs, Will lay sleeping, his small starfish hand tucked up under the dark curls, bright green eyes shuttered against a wicked world. The house was quiet. 'Like the tomb,' the words came unbidden into Leah's mind. It had taken many weeks for the authorities to list the dead and notify the living after the 'Big Push' in July and the sunshine of high summer flooded the room, caught and spun on the copper and the pewter plates. The range gleamed with a heartless cold gleam, the black kettle sizzling away comfortably, and still Leah sat and looked at the envelope. What would it contain? She thought of Billy's body, his beautiful limbs mutilated, his lovely eyes blinded, but, her lips tightened, it would still be Billy, he would come back to her. What if the letter said 'Missing. Presumed dead?' She knew what that meant – nothing left, nothing recognisable of what had once been a human being, no part of Billy's body to grieve over. But dead? Billy dead? Her Billy? How would she bear it? What would she, could she, do? And so she sat looking at the envelope. She felt that she might sit there for ever, never knowing the truth until, upstairs the baby stirred and murmured and she leapt from her seat and snatched the envelope and tore it open. She read the bald message. *We regret to inform you,* in one glance her eyes focusing on the word which told her everything. *Dead*. Billy dead. She threw the envelope away from her in a gesture of despair and a great scream wrenched from her throat, 'Billy. Oh Billy? Where are you?'

A great despairing anger seized her, 'How could you leave me,' she cried, 'all alone.'

Upstairs the baby stirred uneasily at the sound, its little fist clenching and unclenching as Leah's cries echoed through the quiet house. That night, in the cold room she wrote her final letter to Taylor O'Neill. *Billy is dead,* she wrote and again, *Billy is dead*. She underlined the words and tears fell on the black ink and smudged the dreadful words as she put her head on the old oak table and cried until she could cry no more.

★

James was sent home to an army hospital in Sheffield and his wounded body began slowly to heal although his mind was still crowded with the awful sights and sounds of battle. All the while, he kept the lock of hair as a talisman and a link of comradeship with Billy. His dreams were plagued with the battlefield and over and over again, in a grotesque slow motion he saw Billy falling to his knees and his thick blood ooze out of the dreadful wound, saw again Billy's eyes turned to him as if in mute reproach whilst the flies buzzed and gorged on the dreadful wound. He had known without thinking that the lock of hair he had retrieved from Billy had belonged to Leah and the contents of Billy's pocketbook had proved it for in there was a photograph of Leah. She had been smiling at the camera, Will in her arms. It was a stiff and unnatural pose, taken in a studio and yet it had captured her look of love for Billy. James looked at the photo many times. He had almost a mystical feeling that Billy had given Leah to him to look after in expiation of his youthful transgression and knew that when he was well he would return to Cumberland to find her and help her in some tangible way. He knew too that when he was passed as fit and well again he would have to return to the terrible killing fields of war. The news was bad and he would not have long to savour a time without bloodshed.

★

Taylor O'Neill had moved his business to New York. America was growing fat with the spoils of war and he wanted to be in the banking capital of the world. On the way he had acquired a cute little stenographer who was determined to impress him, and if her secret dreams were known, to marry him. During the move, Elspeth, as she was called, had found the ever growing box of letters which had awaited Taylor's attention, and so it was on a late autumn day in his office overlooking the Hudson that Taylor at last read Leah's letters. Elspeth, ever efficient, had arranged the unopened letters in chronological order by the date stamp and he began curiously to read of Leah's life in Caldbeck. Leah had a vivid turn of phrase and a love of words and as he read a picture of Leah was indelibly planted in his mind. The afternoon sun paled and he turned on his desk lamp and still he read. As Leah's letters became more confident and she wrote more freely to him, a picture of her sprang unbidden to his mind and he could recall quite clearly her clear grey eyes and the wonderful hair and the innate pride in her. Her love for Billy and the old man leaped from the page and he smiled as she described Billy's rehiring of her at Cockermouth fair and rejoiced in his heart at her marriage.

He read on into the early evening and as her letters to him became more intimate and she opened up her heart to him in her writing and revealed her inner self to him as she could never have done in his physical presence, he fell in love for the first time in his life. All her honesty and her capacity to love and give, her sensitivity and the beauty of her inner soul jumped off the page and called to him with a clear uncompromising voice. When he opened Leah's last letter and read *Billy is dead. Billy is dead* tears gushed into his eyes and he wept as if for a dear friend and for the love which had been so savagely killed. He sat for a long time in his office, slowly looking round at the trappings of success. No one had loved him as Leah had loved Billy. He had had many women, but hastily, and had given nothing of himself in his search for money and power. Now Leah's voice called to him as clearly and compellingly as if she were in the room and he knew inevitably he would meet her again, that he must go to her and take what life might bring him.

James's body took a long time to heal and it was to be six months of pain before he felt well enough to return home.

His Mother and sister had been to see him several times and had stood white-faced at the end of his bed hardly comprehending that this thin stranger with lines of pain etched on his face and the blank hazel eyes, was James.

As soon as he felt well enough, he wanted desperately to return to Cumberland and to the Hall. He was like a wounded animal which wished to retire to its lair and lick its wounds. In the late February he made the long train journey to Carlisle by train, arriving at the Citadel station, its Victorian scrolled ironwork and glass roof and the rose-pink sandstone façade grimy in the smoke-filled air. He had time to kill before he caught his train which would take him down the coast to Whitehaven and thence to Netherghyll and so he walked outside the station to savour the clear fresh air. On an impulse he hailed a taxi and climbing inside stiffly, he ordered an agreeably surprised driver to take him to Caldbeck village. His spirits lifted as the taxi began the long climb up to Caldbeck and he gazed curiously around him as the panorama of the plain of Carlisle stretched out to his right, the hills of Scotland sharply etched against the clear spring sky, and the fells of Caldbeck and mighty Skiddaw reared upon his left. At last, the taxi made the steep descent into the little village and James ordered it to stop outside the post office-cum-shop. The owner of the village shop greeted him curiously and gave him the directions to Cold Harbour Farm, eager to be rid of him so that she could tell the village of the stranger in uniform going to see Leah. She guessed that he would be someone who had known Billy in the war. All the village mourned some young man, and Billy, with his good looks and insouciant charm had been a favourite. With kindly compassion, trying not to stare at the pale stranger she directed James to the path over the fells which led to the farm. James limped slowly over the rough road to the farm. Now that he had started his journey he was uncertain how to finish it, or indeed what to say when or if he met Leah. His fingers closed instinctively over the lock of hair in the gold clasp which he had in his pocket, always close to him and slid over the smooth leather of Billy's pocketbook which he had brought for Leah. In his pocket he also had his small sketchbook which he had carried to war. Still, he sighed to himself, he had asked the taxi to wait for an hour and he might as well finish what he had started even if he was uncertain of the outcome of his visit.

Leah looked disbelievingly down the fell. The pale sun was in her eyes and she held her hand up against the light, watching the tall uniformed figure make its way slowly and painfully across the fell. It was Billy. Her heart told her it was Billy even though her mind told her it could not be true. Yet only Billy would use the fell paths, she knew only Billy in a Lonsdale uniform.

'Billy!' she screamed, her voice high with excitement and longing.

'Billy.'

She ran stumbling down the path, her eyes blinded by the sun, her arms outstretched. She was in his arms. James held her as if he would never let her go, feeling the pounding of her heart against his chest, all the young warm aroused smell of her in his nostrils, the softness of her glorious hair against his face. They stood for a long moment, close together like lovers until she drew back from him and her hand snaked out to give him a glancing blow to his cheek so strong that he stumbled.

'Who are you?' she called cut in anguish, her face screwed up in pain and anger.

'What are you doing here?' Her face crumpled, 'and why can't you be Billy. Oh, Billy. Billy!' and she began to cry great keening cries as if her heart were truly breaking, as indeed she felt it to be.

James stood there watching not knowing what to do. The blow she had dealt him smarted and he suddenly felt deathly tired. His wounds throbbed from the long walk over the rough path and all at once it was too much to bear, the girl's anguish, Billy's death, his own pain and he sank down on to the cold wet grass as the clear sky darkened around him.

James slowly returned to consciousness and found that he was cradled in Leah's arms, her tears wetting his cheeks.

'I'm sorry,' she moaned softly over and over again, 'I'm sorry. Whoever you are. I'm sorry.'

James lay still for a moment, his eyes closed, savouring the bitter-sweet moment of closeness then stiffly he stood up and stood looking down at her. She was deathly pale and breathing rapidly. He offered her his hand which after a brief hesitation she took and he helped her up until she stood face to face with him. A flare of recognition lit her grey eyes and she shrank away from him.

'Yes,' he said tiredly, 'it is me. But,' he held out the battered pocketbook, 'I've come to give you this.' He held out Billy's pocketbook. Leah took it in disbelief.

'How did you get this?' she asked sharply, her hand closing over the book possessively.

'I was with Billy when he died.'

James answered quietly.

'We lay together on the battlefield.'

His hazel eyes darkened and he swayed slightly, fearful lest he should be overcome with the dreadful memories. Leah looked at him intently and saw his pain and anguish.

'Come with me,' she said softly, 'come to the farm, you need something warm inside you.'

They walked the short distance to the farm in silence. Will was in his pram in the cobbled yard watched over carefully by Lucy, the little servant girl, the ever-present Holly lying watchfully at his side. Leah drew James into the living room and helped him sit in front of the fire. James sat quietly, enjoying the warmth, as Leah brewed some sweet hot tea and gave it to him with a slice of fruit cake. Leah sat and watched him until he was finished and then said simply, 'Tell me.'

James told her everything.

As he talked memories overcame him and he relived the noise and fury of the battle and his voice shook and became hoarse with pent up agony. When he came to Billy's death he bent his head and his words faltered until they tailed off into the silence of the room broken only by the bubble and squeak of the fire. For a long time they sat in silence, each caught up in their thoughts.

'Did he suffer?' Leah asked in anguish.

'No,' James replied quickly, 'it was over in a second.'

'In a second,' she whispered painfully.

'Billy's life over in a second.'

'I must go,' said James, breaking the fragile silence.

'My taxi is waiting down in Caldbeck.'

'Will you come again?' Leah beseeched, 'Please say you'll come again. I need to talk,' her voice broke, 'about Billy.'

'Yes,' he said simply, 'I'll come tomorrow.'

He took her hand for a brief instance and then he passed her his sketchbook. Silently he turned and walked out of the room, through the kitchen out of the yard, to begin his painful walk back over the fells. Leah sat down heavily turning the sketchbook over in her hands, then very carefully she opened it. Images of war starkly met her eyes. Sharp and clear, needing no words, James's sketches told her everything about the long brutal struggle of man against man and the disgusting barbarity of the futility of war. She turned a page and there was Billy in all his beauty, his head thrown back in laughter. She could almost hear his joyous laugh, frozen in time. There he was again, his head bent over a book, his face withdrawn and closed. Another page saw him writing, she guessed to her. She sat and looked at the drawings for a long time then slowly she raised the sketchbook to her lips and very gently kissed the picture of Billy laughing, tears gathering in her luminous grey eyes until at last they trickled down her pale cheeks and fell on the page. She picked up Billy's pocketbook where it lay on the table and caressed the smooth leather. Slowly, she opened it and looked pitifully at the meagre contents. There was a photograph of her and the baby, the photo was cracked and creased as if it had been handled many times and tacked in the flap was an unfinished letter.

My dearest wife, Billy had written, *I am afraid for tomorrow. All I have to protect me is your love and the love of the son I've never seen. Loving you has been the most wonderful experience and I long...'* the writing stopped and a blot of ink, as if mixed with tears stained the page. Leah bent her head over the page, her tears falling on the paper. She looked inside the flap of the pocketbook for the lock of hair she had given Billy, but it was not there.

Betrayal

True to his word, James went back to Caldbeck the next day. Tired and upset, he had arrived back in Carlisle and had wired the Hall that he was 'unavoidably detained' and then wearily booked himself into the Crown and Mitre. The next morning, he again took a taxi to Caldbeck, and for the next two weeks he spent the days with Leah. At first Leah wanted feverishly to talk about the war, and about Billy's death. James knew with a sure instinct that she needed to talk about Billy and his death, to make the unreal a reality and he gently talked about Billy and the sights and sounds of war. Leah had torn the picture of Billy laughing from out of the sketchbook and put it in an old frame on the sandstone mantelpiece and they sat and talked in the quiet room, Leah seeming to gain comfort from her surroundings and their familiarity, her eyes forever straying to the picture of the laughing handsome Billy. James went down the rough track each night to his waiting taxi, feeling empty and drained, but his conversations with Leah had exercised his own demons and each night, he fell fast asleep in his narrow bed, visions of Leah spinning through his head. During the second week, Leah told James of her meeting with Billy at the Hiring Fair and the journey to Caldbeck and the growing love between her and Billy.

'You see,' she said to him one day, her direct grey gaze pinning him to her, 'if it hadn't been for you, Billy and I would never have met.'

It was the first time she had referred to James's connection with the Hall and the events which precipitated her departure. James flushed to the roots of his hair.

'Leah,' he stammered, 'I have regretted my actions ever since. I can only plead,' he said gravely taking her hand in a fit of daring, 'that you were so beautiful...' his voice died away as a burning blush suffused Leah's pale cheeks.

'Enough,' she said hurriedly, 'it is long past... and best forgotten.'

The day came when James knew he must resume his journey to the Hall. He made the journey to Caldbeck with a heavy heart.

Funny, he thought as he walked up the path to the Farm, the old clichés are true. Hearts do feel heavy and they do feel pain. He knew that in his heart his destiny was entwined with Leah. He admired her courage and most of all, yes he admitted to himself he was jealous of the love she felt for Billy, a love that no one as yet had felt for him. He thought of Mary Flanagan and their brief and passionate coupling and then he imagined taking Leah close to him, her body soft and pliant. It was an unseasonably warm day and the sun warmed his body and made him feel alive again after a winter of pain. He rounded a corner on the path, and then he saw her as if in answer to his thoughts. Leah was sitting on the springy turf waiting for him. She was crying as if her heart would break, her hair falling over her face as if to hide her grief. He stopped and gently knelt beside her, tenderly pushing back the soft tendrils of hair.

'Leah,' he said gently, 'what's the matter?'

She turned her pale face towards him, the huge grey eyes almost translucent with tears, 'I don't want you to go,' she sobbed.

James felt his heart, the heart which a few moments ago he had felt to be broken, leap within his breast.

'Oh Leah,' he cried wildly, 'I don't want to go.'

He knelt beside her and held out his arms to her and with a sigh she came to him.

'I am so lonely,' she said softly, as if giving him permission for what was to come. Slowly, James undid the buttons of her blue cotton dress and pulled it gently from her bare shoulders. Gently, slowly, he pulled the dress down to her waist, his breath quickening at the sight of her lovely nakedness, like a sigh in the quiet air. He stood over her and taking her hand he pulled her to her feet. They walked silently off the path and round a curve of the fell hidden from view. Gently, he lowered her to the springy turf as Billy had done so many months before. The sun shone in a clear blue sky and the hum of bees in the heather murmured away the day. Far above, a skylark threw his song to the heavens. Neither spoke, as if in a spell. Leah lay in his arms, her eyes closed, her breathing getting quicker until at last with infinite care, he had undressed her. She lay naked in his arms as he slowly moved his mouth over her breasts and down her body, kissing and caressing her, his fingers moving in her moistness until Leah was aroused and ready. He drew back from her, 'Is this what you want Leah?' he asked wonderingly.

'Yes,' said Leah so quietly he could hardly hear. He undressed as Leah lay watching him, her eyes widening at the long livid scar extending down James's thigh and leg. It made her think of Billy but she stifled the thought. She needed physical love, craved a loving touch, wanted to feel like a woman again. She wanted to feel alive, affirm her being, push away the thought of death and dying. James, gentle James, might never come back and this was all she had to give. The world was far away on the high fells and today might be all she had, all he had, her living link with Billy. James made love to her gently, slowly, his body trembling to be close to her. He came in a surge of ecstasy mingled with grief and pain for he knew that Leah did not, could not love him. Leah's body responded to him, her mind was full of James's body, the warm male smell of him, the feel of her own arousal. She had so missed making love and her whole body had been starved for touch and taste and release from her sorrows. At the moment of fulfilment, she arched her body and cried, 'Billy. Billy!' into the still warm air.

Afterwards, they lay in each others arms, their treacherous bodies still mingled but their thoughts far from each other. Now it was over and passion spent, Leah was deathly ashamed. She felt she had betrayed Billy with a stranger… and yet James was no stranger, he was a link to Billy, her mind spun, she knew she had wanted James to make love to her. James lay beside her. He had taken advantage of her sorrow and need, he could have restrained himself and yet he thought of her passion, her excitement; she had needed him. The thought filled him with joy. They looked deeply into each other's eyes and to Leah's surprise James laughed.

'I cannot feel sad, Leah,' he said firmly, 'we answered the need in each other and there are only the two of us to blame.' Leah relaxed at his laugh.

'I wanted you very much, James,' she confessed. 'It was because…'

'Shush.' He put a gentle finger to her lips, 'I know. I know how you feel.'

'Do you, James?' she asked quietly, a mingled feeling of relief and guilt springing up in her.

'Yes,' he answered slowly, 'I think I do.' He took her into his arms again.

'Will you make love to me this time and not to Billy?' Leah flushed and slowly nodded. This time Leah gave herself to him passionately without reservation, touching him to arouse him, caressing his long lean body, kissing the awful scars until James could contain himself no longer and he rode and thrust her until they both cried out together in the still air. Afterwards, they lay and looked at each other in a kind of awe at the passion they had both felt.

'I think I am falling in love with you,' James said to her, looking in her face to see what answer she would give him. Her hands came up protestingly and her eyes clouded.

'I know,' said James before she could speak, 'you love Billy and it's too soon but I have to go back to France in six weeks and I long to know if you can give me any hope. After all,' he said deliberately, 'Billy is dead and I am alive.'

Leah looked at him aghast at the brutality of his remark and yet her body had just told her that she had acknowledged that Billy would never come back to her. She would have remained faithful for ever if Billy had lived, she knew. She would never have looked at another man if her Billy had not been... she used the word to herself for the first time... dead.

'I am going to the Hall tomorrow,' said James gently. 'I can delay no longer. There is business to look after and my Mother needs me. But if you allow it, I will come and see you before I return to France.'

Leah nodded, unable to speak any words of comfort to him. It was a high blue day and they walked a long way over the springy turf on the fells. The lakeland hills were hazy in the heat and above their heads the reckless skylark spun its skeins of sound into the clear air.

'It's hard to believe that men are still killing each other and that the war still continues,' said James sombrely.

Leah shuddered, 'Must you return, James?' she asked slowly, 'Surely you've done enough?'

'There's still more to do,' replied James sadly, 'I have to return in six weeks time.'

'Oh James,' she cried sadly, 'you have spent so much time with me when you should have been with your family. What will they think?'

'Leah,' said James slowly, 'these last two weeks, sad though they have been for you, have given me new purpose. I have had no one to fight for till now. Now I shall think of you and Will and the high fells and it will give me sanity and a reason to survive.' He stopped hurriedly, fearful that his words would startle her, for they came from the depths of his heart. He was closer to her than to any other living person, even Mary Flanagan whom he had lain with in the heat of battle.

'Leah.' He put out his hand and took hers in his.

'May I see you again? We have become more than friends yet less than lovers and I believe in my heart that somehow we were meant to meet and have our lives entwined.'

Leah gave a protesting cry but he continued.

'Leah. I know you cannot even feel anything for me, so great was your love for Billy, but can we at least be friends... and can I return to you, if only as a friend?'

Leah sat for a long moment, her hand steady in his. His auburn hair had grown during the last two weeks and flopped into his eyes, hazel eyes which looked at her with such warmth the ice round her heart began to melt. He looked so young, she caught a look of the boy she remembered and yet his face was marked with suffering, and pity suffused her. It was a small thing to say 'Yes' to someone who might never return. She smiled steadily at him,

'Yes, James,' she said at last, 'we are friends already and will remain friends till your return.'

Seeing the look of longing in his eyes she leaned towards him and put her small rough hand on his cheek in a somehow maternal gesture, and then moved by pity and tenderness she moved towards him and kissed him gently on the mouth. He held her close as something fragile and precious, immeasurably moved by the gesture and for a long moment the war was forgotten by them both.

Lizzie

James found the Hall greatly changed on his return. The long drive up to the Hall was unkempt and overgrown and a general air of neglect pervaded the atmosphere. Inside the Hall the same feel of emptiness and decay hit him. The long windows were dusty and streaked and the stiff folds of the brocade curtains hung with dust. His Mother too had changed. Her fine dark looks had vanished and her face was thin and weary.

'It isn't that we lack the money, James,' she said sharply after James had made brief comment at the changes.

'Your Father left me well provided for. We just can't get the servants. The men are away and the women too busy playing at being men to want to come and look after the Hall. They prefer to be in shops or offices. Even Flora has chosen to live in Whitehaven and work in the library rather than stay here.' James was surprised to hear that Flora had deigned to work, but kept silent.

'Only Lizzie has stayed to care for us,' his Mother continued, 'she does everything for me.'

Lizzie had grown into a sullen, dull-looking woman. Mrs Hodgson, the cook, had died and Lizzie had taken over her duties. The food was plain yet edible but Lizzie's manner was grudging and her attitude to James's Mother was proprietorial. James spoke to her one day in the breakfast room before his Mother had joined him.

'Your friend, Leah,' he broached the subject, 'do you remember her?'

'Aye. Ah do indeed,' Lizzie replied darkly.

'Her husband was in my regiment,' James told her, 'he was killed. I...' He stopped, seeing a flash of jealously cross Lizzie's face and then continued slowly, 'I had to go and see her. She lives on Caldbeck. I thought you might like to know where she is,' he ended slowly, seeing her face visibly darken.

'No Mr James,' she said vindictively.

'Ah would not like to know. Ah know why she left here,' she shot him a sly look full of venom, 'and ah didn't like the way she carried on wid that American either,' she almost spat the words.

James felt as if he had been stabbed by her words. Leah and the American? He remembered Taylor with affection, and his mind raced at the implication in Lizzie's remarks.

'That American?' James asked in bewilderment.

'Aye. Allus sending her notes,' Lizzie replied, embroidering the truth in her jealousy. James turned away from her, lest she see the hurt she had caused, little knowing that it would be all over the village that night that, 'Mister James was seeing that Leah Fletcher who had left in disgrace years ago.'

James's time at the Hall was brief, and that pleased him. He had little to say to his Mother, his experiences in the War had so changed him and were such that he could not share them with her. He followed up his business as best he could, but the war had changed everything and he knew with a sick heart that should he return he would have much to sort out. He went to see Flora in Whitehaven and he greeted her pleasantly enough, but he was to find as so many soldiers returning found, that he no longer fitted in easily, that his place in society had changed and that home and country would never be the same again. However kind and pleasant his uncles were and his Mother's friends, a whole strata of his youthful friends and relations had been swallowed up by the war and those left behind had no conception of the living hell he was shortly to return to. He held his Mother close as he said his goodbyes and was amazed to feel her thin frame shudder with tears.

'I don't know what to say to you lad,' she said lapsing into Cumbrian, 'you are so precious to me. Come back safe.'

She clung to him and sobbed uncontrollably. James was immeasurably moved by her words. He had never been close to her yet she was all he had. He dried her tears kindly with his handkerchief.

'Mother,' he said regretfully, 'I know my leave has not been a happy time for us, but there are things I cannot share. The War...' he choked on the words.

'Aye lad,' she said softly, 'it has changed all our hopes and dreams. All our futures. But,' she stiffened, 'I care nowt for that. Just come home and we can start anew.'

James hugged her thin frame, moved by her words and unguessed at affection. During the long train ride to Carlisle, along the coast from Whitehaven to Workington and Maryport and then to Wigton and Carlisle, he thought of his past, his privileged past and of the changes now apparent. He did not care for privilege. Being in the Army had taught him that a man was a man and as brave as he wherever he had come from, he still had the same needs and longings. On his arrival at Carlisle, he thought briefly of going to see Leah but Lizzie's words had soured him and clouded his feelings. His mind was full of doubt about her. He thought of their lovemaking under the blue sky and then thought of Billy. Always Billy. He knew that she had thought of Billy the first time they made love, just as he knew the second time had been for him alone. Yet she had been so eager for lovemaking, so hot for passion. He thought of her swimming naked, and then jealous thoughts of Taylor O'Neill flashed into his head. Maybe the American had seen her also. Maybe… the thoughts in his tired brain hurt his head. What was the point in going to see her if she still loved Billy… and yet how quickly she had let him make love to her the insidious voice in his head whispered. Maybe all he had thought about her from the first moment he met her was wrong, based on his boyish dreams of her naked body. Instead he wearily caught the train which would take him to London for his orders and which would then take him back to the front and the desperate struggle still going on.

Baby

In the few weeks that James was at the Hall, Leah knew incontrovertibly that she carried James's child. She was in a panic. She had waited for some sign from him, a letter, a visit, a postcard, some sign that he existed and had some feeling for her, but as the weeks went by she increasingly despaired. A child. Out of wedlock. ('A bastard.') So soon after Billy's death. She relived her passionate lovemaking with James. ('Lovemaking? Animal coupling.') She blushed with shame. Maybe he had wanted to fulfil his fantasies begun at Netherghyll Hall so many years ago. The old shame came back to haunt her. Maybe he had just needed a woman's body as she had needed a man's body close to her, affirming her youth, affirming the feeling of being alive. She thought of them lying naked under the wide sky ('For all to see.') Bile rose in her throat. How free she had been with her body and now she must pay for her sins. In some peculiar way she had found their lovemaking a link with Billy.

'Oh Billy,' she moaned aloud, 'how could I do this? Why did you leave me?'

She had existed in a limbo of half feeling since Billy's death. She had wanted James physically, and not thought of consequences. She surveyed her treacherous lovely body in the mirror. Nothing showed yet of the child to come. Her body was still slim and lovely, the pale pearly skin looked virginal and perfect. She knew she could not stay in Caldbeck. The shame would be too much, Billy had been a

148

local hero. Anyway, she acknowledged that she could not run the Farm. Billy's uncle had indicated his interest. In ordinary times, she would have rented it out until Will was old enough to decide what to do; she knew however, that now her life was changing, changed by a moment of passion. Still, she thought she would wait for another week, just another week. She knew not what she was waiting for. She spent her days with Will, holding him to her frequently. She did not want another man's child. Time hung loosely round her like a shroud.

★

James was miserable. The war was going badly and men, particularly officers like himself, were needed to fill the gaps in the trenches. He waited for his orders. He knew he had behaved badly towards Leah, leaving her without a word or even a note. Making love to her, whatever his feelings now, had been a heart-stopping experience for him. He thought of her constantly, of her beautiful body yielding to his, although he knew that her first passion had been an affirmation of her love for Billy, he remembered the exultation of their second coupling when she had responded to him alone and he had ridden her to fulfilment. He thought of Lizzie and her fat vindictive face and began to question her sly innuendoes and as he did so, he began to feel a change of heart towards Leah. He thought of her love for Billy, her loneliness, and the image of Billy lying on the battlefield returned to haunt his dreams. Billy's outstretched hand mutely appealed to him for help. He felt ashamed that he had denied Billy a peaceful end and was ashamed of the way he had treated Billy's wife. Images of her face and the pain-filled grey eyes consumed him and seemed to burn into his soul. One day as he absently pulled his cigarette case out of his pocket, the lock of blonde hair fell out and he knew with a blinding flash that he must see her again before he returned to the ghastly war and to what seemed certain death.

★

And so it was, one glorious May Day, only a week after his return to London, that James once more toiled up the path to Caldbeck after the seemingly interminable journey back to Cumberland. All seemed deserted at the Farm as he walked through the cobbled yard to the kitchen, then Holly catapulted through the kitchen door closely followed by Will and then by Leah herself. She had lost weight and her face was pale, her eyes huge in her white face. She stood and looked at him without speaking then swayed slightly. James moved swiftly towards her.

'Leah,' he cried 'what's wrong? Are you ill?' He unconsciously put out a hand to hold her Leah looked at him and seeing the overriding concern and alarm in his face answered with dignity.

'I am not ill, James. I am carrying your child.'

He caught his breath in amazement and then moved forward and took both of her hands in his. They trembled within his grasp and he was overcome with a powerful wave of feeling. Now that he had seen her, all his doubts were swept away and all that he had felt for her came flooding back. How could he have doubted her? One look at her face told him of the sadness and anguish she had felt at his betrayal.

'Hush, Leah,' he said softly and held her in his arms and soothed her as he would a child. 'It will be all right, it will be all right,' he whispered over and over again. Leah began to cry and very gently he stroked the white blonde hair, silky underneath his touch. She laid her head against his chest.

'I thought you had gone for ever,' she confessed.

'Would you have cared?' The words were torn out of him unwillingly.

'Yes, James,' she replied simply, 'I would have cared.'

He held her close and told her everything about his visit to the Hall, of the change in his Mother, of Lizzie's barbed comments, of his jealousy, of his doubts. Without a word, she drew him into the house and to her desk. She took out Taylor's letter, his one and only letter, and showed it to James. James read it, ashamed of his base thoughts.

'In all my life, Taylor has been my true friend and companion.'

She told him of her weekly letters to Taylor and how he had become her absent friend; she told him of the books she had bought with Taylor's money, and of how she had taught Billy to read and opened up their minds.

'Will you, can you forgive me?' James asked desperately. All that had happened to this girl had been at his doing and Taylor had been a friend whereas all he had done was seduce her. He thought of the handsome, simple Billy and tears filled his eyes.

'Oh yes, James,' she faltered, 'we have had a bad beginning for people who have been,' she paused, 'so close to one another.'

'A baby,' he said dazedly, 'a baby.'

He did not question that it was his. His doubts had vanished to be replaced with the certainty that they were meant to be together and a feeling of joy that he and this lovely girl in a moment of passion should produce a child.

'We must marry right away, Leah,' he demanded joyously.

'You must not marry me out of pity,' she countered furiously. 'I can manage. I have sold the farm and am moving away. No one will know of the child.'

'You must not be ashamed of our child!' James said passionately. 'It was born in a moment of loneliness for us both but it deserves, it will get,' he added firmly, 'a lifetime of love.'

He silenced her protests with his arguments. 'I cannot go to War and leave a bastard behind me.' Leah shrank from the fierceness of his words.

'My child shall have its inheritance should I not return. I know you care for me a little, Leah,' he said simply, 'you would not have made love with me otherwise.'

Leah blushed to the roots of her hair.

'I feel for you and our child. Let me care for you. Give you the protection of my name. If I return and you are not happy, we can divorce. Marry me. Give the child a name and yourself a husband. Many a marriage has started off with less than this.'

Worn out with his arguments and numbly content to find some sort of salvation, Leah agreed to marry James, and the next day in Carlisle Registry Office in front of two disinterested and unknown witnesses, James and Leah became man and wife, with little Will holding on to both their hands. Leah shuddered superstitiously as she repeated the words 'Till Death us do part' remembering her first marriage and her vows to Billy.

Leah walked with James to the Citadel Railway Station, Will prattling at her knee. There was no time for a honeymoon for James had to be in London that day. He looked at her soberly as they waited for his train in the great arching glass canopy of the station.

'Till Death us do part, Leah. If I return I shall be the best husband ever.'

He saw a shadow cross her face.

'I know you can never forget Billy but we and the children have everything to live for. A new beginning after this dreadful war.'

He was determined to phone his solicitor on his arrival in London so that he might change his will and leave everything to Leah and the unborn child. With a belch of rancid smoke and a great iron gasp, the train drew into the station. Its engine haemorrhaging steam into the vaulted cathedral-like roof. James leaned out of the window.

'Write to me soon, Leah,' he commanded, 'let me know what is happening and where you are.' His hand touched her hair briefly then he suddenly put his hand in his pocket and pulled out the lock of hair, the gold clasp gleaming in the grey filtered light.

'I have this to protect me.'

Leah's face blanched in horror. It was the lock of hair she had given Billy to take to war. James could only have got it from Billy's dead body. She shuddered and moved away but the train was already pulling away from the station. She stood rigid until the train moved round the long curve of the track and out of sight of the station. A feeling of dread overcame her and she had to sit down, suddenly, on a bench. Will pulled impatiently at her hand. She sat there for long while. She was a married woman again, she had things to do. First of all she had to tell her Mother of her hurried marriage. Her Mother already knew that James had been to see her and had been not entirely reconciled to their meeting, despite James's link with Billy. Leah stood up, her back stiffening, and walked down the long platform and over the bridge without looking back.

*

'How could you, Leah?' Hannah demanded, her face white with shock. Leah had never seen her Mother angry in all her life and stood in front of her like a frightened schoolgirl, her head bent, her arms at her sides. Wilson Beck stood ramrod stiff by the sandstone lintel, his face grim with displeasure. Leah had telephoned them from Carlisle asking them as a matter of urgency to make the long journey through to see her. They had driven as quickly as Wilson Beck's cautious driving would allow.

'A baby. To James Forbes Robertson.'

Hannah's brain reeled at the thought of the scandal to come, 'And to marry him, so soon after...' Her voice shook with outrage.

'So soon after Billy's death,' Leah finished for her, 'You cannot say anything to me that I have not already said. You cannot accuse me of any more disloyalty than I have accused myself. I have scourged myself at my disloyalty to Billy for a moment of comfort.'

'Many women are left alone,' said Wilson Beck sombrely, 'but they do not get pregnant.'

'I don't want this baby,' screamed Leah suddenly, 'I hate the thought of it in my body,' she struck herself a tremendous blow with her clenched fist, 'I wish it were dead.'

She stopped suddenly at the enormity of what she had said. The baby had not asked to be born. Leah's scream affected Hannah.

'Oh, do not wish it dead, Leah,' she cried desperately.

'Poor little thing. We will manage.' She took Leah into her arms like a child and held her close, smoothing her hair. Her daughter, her darling daughter, and another little child to love. She smiled mistily, maybe it wasn't so bad. Many a woman had ended up in the same situation.

'I didn't know what to do,' Leah sobbed, 'the child a bastard. Oh, Billy, Billy,' she cried as if her heart would break, 'Why did you leave me? I love you so.

'Hush child,' Hannah comforted compassionately, 'it will be all right.'

She looked over Leah's head to Wilson Beck and he smiled and put his hand out to hers in a gesture of support.

Allonby

It was agreed that Billy's uncle would buy the Farm as quickly as possible, so that he might make arrangements over the winter for the new lambing cycle in spring. Wilson Beck had proved a tower of strength and had insisted to Leah that he would make arrangements for her. All Leah stipulated was that she needed somewhere to live which was quiet and where, no one would know her. In just over a week, Leah and Will set off in Wilson Beck's car for a new life.

Leah was now a rich woman, for the Farm covered many acres of pastureland. She left the Farm without a backward glance. She could not bear to look as the car drew up the steep hill out of Caldbeck. She had been so happy there until Billy's death. She felt as if she were exiling herself from all which was secure and loved. The whole village was agog at her precipitate departure but all agreed that Leah could not manage the farm herself and none guessed at the underlying reason for her going. The car followed the rough road to Wigton, the road down which she and Billy had driven in the trap so many years ago when she had bought presents for him and his Father. She thought of Billy, his laugh, his passionate love for her, teaching him to read on the rosy winter's nights and tears came to her eyes. What would have life been with no War? Living with Billy in the natural circle of their life, farming their land. The phrase 'Till Death us do part' flashed into her mind and made her think of James and the child within her. Her face stiffened and she brushed the tears away from her eyes. This was her new life, like it or not, fate and her own unruly emotions had carved the way for it.

The journey continued almost as far as Maryport, a little bustling town with a thriving fishing fleet and a harbour, prosperous with the coal trade. The car took a sharp right turn along the coast road to Allonby. Wilson Beck had bought Leah a little cottage looking over the green to the sea. It had a small forecourt garden and a larger garden at the back. It was dusk as Leah walked up the path cobbled with sea-washed pebbles, an anchor in white pebbles worked in amongst them. Sandstone steps rose to a bright green painted front door with a brass knocker shaped like a dolphin. The door was ajar and led into a small vestibule. A coloured glass door with leaded panes depicting a highly coloured phoenix opened into the small hall. Her Mother came bustling out to meet them.

'Leah!' she hugged her daughter, 'and Will.' Stooping she gave Will a kiss as Lucy came out of the kitchen and took Will away for a warming drink.

'Come.' She drew Leah into a small parlour, brightly lit with gas lamps. Leah cried out in pleasure. A bright fire shone in the marble grate and comfortable well upholstered armchairs pulled up in front of it. The rag rug from Caldbeck was laid on a green carpet, and sitting on it as if she had been there forever was Holly. A few pictures from the farm were scattered on the white walls and copper and pewter from the farm winked and twinkled from the beams as if they had always been so. Green velvet curtains on mahogany poles hung in front of the wide windows. Leah cried, 'Mother. It's perfect. I know I shall be happy here.'

The warmth and charm of the place wrapped themselves round her and her cold heart warmed with an unexpected glow. She knelt down in front of the fire and patted Holly who immediately rolled on her back in agonies of joy. She warmed her hands at the inviting fire, then calling Will she went to explore the rest of the house. There was a tiny dining room, waiting for furniture, and a fairly big kitchen with a lit range; this would be Lucy's domain. Upstairs on the first floor was a bathroom with a white bath and wash basin with brass fittings and, wonder of wonders, a toilet, for the previous owner, a retired sea captain had liked his comfort and had no desire to go out of his snug little house to perform his ablutions in a draughty privy in the yard. There were two bedrooms, sparsely furnished for her and Will. At the top of a crooked little staircase were two more bedrooms and, wonder of wonders, another bathroom for Lucy. It was perfect.

'I will send a car for you tomorrow,' said Wilson Beck and, 'you and your Mother can do some shopping in Maryport or Workington for furniture that you might need. We are staying in the Golden Lion at Maryport tonight to be near you.'

Leah accepted the offer gladly, and looked round in a daze of happiness. Her own home, hers to do as she wished.

'I will be happy here,' she repeated firmly, clasping her hands protectively round her slightly swelling stomach. God knows how long it would be before James returned when she would have to make more decisions about her future. Until then, she would be happy waiting for her baby. She had grown to love the child within her and longed to hold it and care for it in reparation for her wild words to Hannah and Wilson Beck.

Allonby was a little fishing village about seven miles from Maryport. It faced west and looked directly on to the setting sun. Over the Solway was Scotland, easily seen. There was a small stone mission, a school, several small shops and a straggle of cottages, houses and farms. No one was curious about Leah, young women on their own with a child were, alas, a common sight in these days of war. People were friendly and soon accepted Leah as part of the small community.

For the next couple of weeks, Leah took advantage of Wilson Beck's offer and she and her Mother indulged in an orgy of shopping for 'Shamrock Cottage'. Both Leah and her Mother enjoyed these outings and secretly thought of the twists of fate which had made them both rich women. Leah had written to James telling him of the move but as yet had heard nothing from him. She knew, for he had told her, that he would have written to his Mother telling her of the marriage and at the moment she was content to let things happen around her and nest in her little cottage. Will was happy too, too young to be curious about the change in his life. He and Lucy and Holly spent hours on the beach looking for shells and sea-washed glass and watching the fishing boats or the dirty little coasters sailing up the Solway to Silloth. Leah, too, was happy in a passive way. She had grown accustomed to the child in her womb and talked aloud to it often. Each day she took a long walk along the green banks or on the deserted sandy shores and her paleness began to vanish and she felt stronger and energetic.

She had seen a doctor in Maryport, an old-fashioned gentleman, singly incurious, who had assured her that she and the child were doing well and that he would make arrangements well before her time was due, in six months. For the moment, she was happy in an undemanding way. After all the emotions of the last year, it was pleasant to have a calm time just for herself. The days seemed to flow effortlessly along and the pain in her heart began to diminish. She still thought of Billy constantly but the ache and the grinding sense of loss had begun to ease. She barely thought of James and if she did it was as if he was a figment of her imagination.

Her horror at seeing James with the lock of hair she had given to Billy had not diminished and was still sharp in her mind, and it coloured any feelings for him she might have had. Her only feelings, she told herself, were regret at their lovemaking and it made her doubly determined to love their child and make it happy.

At the end of the summer she had a visitor. A car drew up in front of the bright green door and a woman got out. She turned and paid the driver and in a clear firm voice bade him to return in an hour, then she walked up the cobbled path and knocked hesitantly on the front door with the dolphin knocker. Leah had just wakened from her afternoon nap and was dressing. She heard the voice asking for Mrs Forbes Robertson. She looked in the mirror to check her appearance. She had put on a little weight, which suited her. Her skin was smooth and brown and her luminous grey eyes were enhanced by the cream lace collar of the fine grey silk dress she wore. She smoothed her shining hair caught in an elegant chignon at the nape of her neck and went unhurriedly downstairs. She gave a cry as she entered the little parlour, for the woman who turned to meet her was Flora Forbes Robertson.

Flora

Leah looked at Flora in silence. How many times had she dreamed about that proud and wilful face? How many times had she shamefully remembered Flora's spite towards her. The silence lengthened as Flora endured Leah's scrutiny. Her face was old before its time, the once fine dark eyes hollow and sad, lines of sorrow etched her face. The dark hair, luxurious no longer and streaked with grey was bundled up untidily under a shapeless hat, her shoulders stooped underneath her fine coat.

'Leah,' her voice was sharp with desperation, 'please do not turn me away. I have come first of all to apologise to you. I am so ashamed at the way I, we, treated you. You did not deserve such shame.'

Leah kept silent and Flora repeated, 'I have bitterly regretted how ill I used you. Please forgive me Leah.' Her voice cracked and Leah saw that she was near to tears. How long ago it all seemed, how unimportant now in her life.

'Hush,' she said after a pause putting a kind hand on Flora's arm, 'it is all so long ago Flora. Yes. I do forgive you. You were young and thoughtless and privileged,' she added as an afterthought.

'Thank you, Leah,' said Flora with dignity, 'you are very kind.' She passed a weary hand over her eyes to disguise her tears, 'Let us have some tea,' suggested Leah to ease the tension. She rang for Lucy and soon the two women were seated opposite each other in front of the fire partaking of Lucy's fresh scones and home-made jam.

'When we received James's letter telling of your marriage, I was determined to seek you out,' Flora explained, 'James told us everything of how he met you again after,' she paused awkwardly, 'your husband's death.' Leah laid her hands on the swell of the child, visible under the grey silk. The baby moved beneath her hands as if sensing her distress, almost taking her breath away.

'James is so overjoyed at the baby,' Flora continued.

'What of your Mother?' Leah interrupted, 'I am sure that she will not be pleased at your brother's marriage to me.'

'My Mother is dead,' Flora said simply. 'She died very suddenly two weeks ago,' her voice broke, 'she and I had only recently made contact with each other again after a long silence. You see,' she smiled wanly, 'I married beneath me.'

'What?' Leah was full of amazement. Flora? The proud and wilful Flora marrying beneath her?

'What of Simon Forrester?' she asked curiously.

'Dead,' said Flora simply. 'Just after the beginning of the War. Somehow nothing seemed to matter after that – all of the silly things we had been brought up to believe and expect, they were all swept away. All my friends were being killed,' she stopped, 'it was more than I could bear. I went to Whitehaven, somehow in my silliness,' she managed a giggle, 'I felt it would help the war effort, and there I met Jackson,' her voice softened. 'He was the loveliest man I had ever seen in my whole life.' Her voice lightened, 'I pursued him unashamedly until he caught me. He owned the chandler's shop in Tangier Street.'

'A shopkeeper?' Leah echoed in amazement. 'You married a shopkeeper?'

Flora looked at her.

'Somehow it did not seem to matter,' Flora said simply, 'he loved me and I loved him. When the war took a turn for the worse, I knew he would volunteer and so I asked him to marry me.' She finished, smiling at her own audacity.

'We were together for just three months and then he went to war.' She bent her head, 'I have not heard from him for a long time. I do not know if he is alive or dead. Needless to say,' she rushed on seeing Leah's look of pity, 'my Mother was not in accord with the match. She had, she said, groomed me for something better than life with a shopkeeper. You know that my Father is dead,' Flora said quietly, 'so you see, Leah, I am almost completely alone. I have let the chandler's shop and am living alone at the Hall until James and you make your home there. At least after Mother's death I have some money. It is a sad place now,' she reflected, 'overrun and neglected. There is no one now who wishes to work there any more. My Mother and I were reconciled before her death,' she added as an afterthought, 'but I think this war had broken her heart as it has broken so many others.'

She stopped and gazed sombrely into the fire. Impulsively, Leah crossed to her and put her arms round her.

'Let us be friends Flora,' she asked, 'we have gone through so much in such a short time. I do not wish to return to the Hall although I suppose I must when James returns. It would make him happy if he thought that we are friends.'

Flora returned her embrace happily.

'You are a good person, Leah,' she whispered. 'Thank you.'

When the car returned for Flora they parted like old friends, each happy that old wounds could heal.

'Please come again, Flora,' Leah begged as Flora stood at the door ready to make her farewell. After the car had turned out of sight round the bend of the road, Leah went back into the bright little parlour with its blazing fire and sat for a long time staring into the flames, looking back over the years of pain and loss and the changes which had brought her and Flora Forbes Robertson together as equals.

Loss

Leah lost the baby one wild autumn night. All day the wind had howled across a sea as grey and dull as steel. The sky was low and huge-bellied grey clouds scudded and tore overhead. The capricious gale picked up and tossed driftwood and pebbles and sand over the green springy turf, across the road on to the paths of the little cottages facing its fury. Leah and Will had spent the day in the bright little cottage, the oil lamps lit prematurely to ward off the gloom. Leah had been restless all day, as if with the premonition of some unspecified disaster. She had never thought of the unborn child, she felt too well. She ascribed her restlessness to the enforced confinement and tried to mask her feelings by playing games with Will and amusing him, but the feeling remained with her all day. That night, as she lay in bed listening to the dull pounding of the waves on the beach and the restless susurration of the sand and pebbles, she thought about her soon to be born child. Would it be a daughter or a son? She hoped for a daughter. A little fair-haired daughter. Her mouth curved into a soft smile as she fell asleep listening to the rain spattering on the tiles and tapping on the window panes. She woke in the dark. The storm coiled and heaved round the cottage like a mad thing. Reaching out, she lit the oil lamp then the pain hit her. A wrenching tearing pain so severe she thought she was dying. She stumbled out of bed to the door, to feel wetness engulf her. Looking down she saw that her cotton night-dress was scarlet with blood. Wrenching open her door she had time to scream, 'Lucy!' before the rushing of her senses mingled with the shriek of the wind and she fell into a dark and scarlet nightmare of pain.

By the time the doctor from Maryport had been roused and reached her after a nightmarish journey along the narrow coast road, Leah had lost her child. It was a girl. She lay rigid in her bed as the doctor fussed around her and Lucy stood white-faced at the door. Will had been taken to a kind neighbour. The gale was abating and cold clear morning light pushed away the darkness as the oil lamp flickered and fussed. Leah turned her face to the wall and cried as if she would never stop. She cried for herself and for Billy and for James but most of all she cried for the child she had grown to love, the little daughter she would never hold in her loving arms. She heard ringing in her ears, her dreadful cry, 'I wish the child were dead.' Well, now the child was dead. She had killed her. Her child.

Hannah and Wilson Beck came as quickly as Wilson could drive the twisting roads and Hannah stayed to look after Leah for several weeks. Leah was unapproachable. She seemed to be in a world which no one could reach. Will grew dismayed and frightened of Leah's strange silence and pale face and took to spending time with Lucy. Hannah watched and grieved, incapable of reaching Leah and eventually, feeling she could do no more, she returned to Workington and to Wilson Beck who seemed to need her more. Before she left she tried to speak to Leah and recapture their closeness.

'Leah dear,' she said pityingly, trying to hold Leah's stiff unyielding body close to hers as if to warm it, 'many women have miscarriages. You will be able to have more children in time.' Leah pulled away from her and gazed at her with pain-filled grey eyes, huge in her pale thin face.

'I wished the child dead,' she whispered, 'and now it is. I killed it.'

Spring

Taylor blew into Leah's life on the back of a spring gale. The cold fresh rain dappled the new buds and the sky was a never-ending blue. The Solway tossed and sparkled in good humour and the coast of Scotland was clearly etched across the lively water. The air seemed warmer and along the green and sandy banks stretching along the coast from Maryport to Allonby was a cerulean haze of bluebells. Leah walked alone on the springy green turf which curved beside the sea. Christmas had come and gone in a haze of pain which never left her. She and Will had stayed in the Becks' comfortable Stainburn house in the fashionable side of Workington. Lucy had happily returned to her family for the holiday, affectionately kissing a protesting Will and bidding him to, 'Have a lovely Christmas.' Rachel, Brian and her family were there on Boxing Day. Rachel was as sweet as ever but Leah could not respond to her kindness and affection. Becks' Groceries was doing well and Wilson now had warehouses to further enrich his assets and his sister and her husband, who were still working in the business, were enjoying the success. Hannah tried to make Christmas as pleasant as she could. It all focused on Will and Rachel's children and there were lots of treats for them including a visit to the circus. Will was happy, and Leah, through a mist of pain was pleased to see him so, but she took no active part in the celebrations. Wilson Beck was a wise man.

'Leave her be, Hannah,' he said to his worrying wife. 'The girl needs to grieve. Time will heal, you will see.'

Now they were back at Allonby. Will had elected to play with his friends under Lucy's ever watchful eye and so Leah walked alone. The early sun warmed her and somewhere inside like a tiny green shoot, something unfurled and her life seemed a little more bearable. She turned to look at the bluebell banks and there he was. He stood and looked at her for a long moment, this woman he had come so far to see. Taller than he remembered, her clear grey eyes seemed transparent, the black fringe of her eyelashes seemed to make the grey like clear glass. She was bare headed and her glorious hair was pinned high on her head like a crown. The breeze had tossed little tendrils which hung like silk against her pale cheeks. Her mouth was softly curved, pink and voluptuous and he had an almost overwhelming desire to press his lips to hers and feed on that softness. She raised a gloved hand to her breast in surprise, the soft curve swelled against the gabardine of her coat. She looked as fresh as the day itself and Taylor was stunned with the rush of feeling he felt for her. Leah looked at him in turn, recognising him instantly. He was tall, much taller than she, and she had to look up to see his face. His patrician good looks were startling, the intensely blue eyes smiled down at her from a smooth tanned face, the straight determined nose and the firm mouth with a slight curve at the side completed a very handsome face. He was a slim build but the shoulders under the expensive coat were broad. He held out a hand to her. The fingers were long and the nails well cared for.

'Leah,' he said in his clipped Bostonian accent, 'at last.'

His voice was as deep and warm as honey. He could hardly believe they were meeting at last. When news of Billy's death came, he had waited for more letters from her. When none came, he had determined somehow to find her.

Now that he had the sight of her, it almost took his breath away. He had instructed an amazed Elspeth to book his passage on the excuse of business in Europe, convincing himself this was only a holiday but hoping in his heart that he would find the girl who had written him such extraordinary letters of such intimacy.

'Dammit,' he said to himself, 'let fate take its course.' He had driven to Caldbeck and managed to persuade the curious lady in the post office to tell him something about Leah. ('Such a lovely girl.')

His search had led him to the Becks. Hannah remembered him instantly for Leah had told her of the money, and Wilson Beck, who was a good judge of character, had given Taylor instructions as to how to find Leah. Wilson Beck had not spoken with Taylor about Leah's marriage to James or of Billy's tragic death. He had enjoyed the other man's company and his searching questions as to the War and its effect.

For a long heart-stopping moment they gazed at each other. Into Leah's mind flooded the thought of the intimacies she had written to this man and somehow he did not seem a stranger. She realised with a flash of revelation that the image of him had always been locked intensely in her memory. What would he think of her? Why was he here? Taylor interpreted the look correctly and broke the awkward moment.

'Come, Leah,' he said and taking her hand firmly in his he tucked it into the curve of his arm and they walked back in silence to the cottage. Outside the cottage stood an enormous black shiny car, the silver mascot gleaming proudly in the sun seeming to float in the air. There was already a small admiring crowd around it. Leah gasped in amazement.

'What is that?' she asked in astonishment.

'That, dear Leah, is a Rolls Royce,' Taylor announced proudly, 'I am hoping that in it we two, if that is all right,' he added anxiously, 'might see something of your lovely county.'

Leah nodded dumbly in assent. Later in the parlour, whilst they were having tea, Taylor told Leah of his visit. He disguised it as 'Business' for he did not want to startle her by any intimacy.

'Tell me about Billy,' he asked gently, 'I know you loved him very much.'

There was a silence, then Leah started to tell him of Billy's death and the aftermath of her meeting with James. When she told him of the hurried marriage, his face darkened. In all his imaginings he had never imagined her married. He knew of her deep love for Billy and he felt disgust at James for taking advantage of Leah's hurt and loneliness. When Leah began to tell Taylor of the death of her baby she began to sob uncontrollably, tears flooding from the grey eyes down her cheeks. Taylor longed to hold her and soothe her but instead he took her hand and held it tightly until the storm had passed. He handed Leah his linen handkerchief and kept silent as she dried her eyes. Hushing her apologies, he leaned towards her and said gently, 'Leah. We have always been friends. When you were a little housemaid at Netherghyll and stood in the breakfast room waiting on me there was always a spark between us. I saw your eyes whilst the Captain and I were talking and knew that you believed in the same things as I. Freedom and dignity.'

Leah looked him straight in the eye, her grey eyes glowing. 'It's true, isn't it?' Taylor insisted.

'You have written to me like a friend and now we meet again. Let us enjoy each other's company whilst I am here, as friends.'

Leah was silent, remembering her time at the Hall and the manner of her dismissal. Taylor had been right and now the world was changed.

The Hall was crumbling and the old ways with it. People were no longer prepared to be servants. Men like Wilson Beck were prospering whilst she was now a rich woman, and the once proud Flora living in a reduced state. All in the space of a few turbulent years. She left her hand lying in Taylor's, enjoying the feeling of protection it gave her and smiled shakily at him.

'You are right, Taylor,' she said wistfully, 'we have always been friends despite oceans dividing us,' and she told him how she had used his money, going to the book case to show him all the books she had bought, talking enthusiastically about the ones she had enjoyed. She told him of teaching Billy to read in the long winter nights at the farm. How long ago it all seemed now. On safer ground they talked about books and the conversation was general until it was time for Taylor to leave. As he took his leave, Taylor took her hand to his lips and kissed it. He told her that he had booked into the Golden Lion in Maryport for four or maybe five weeks, business permitting. Could he prevail upon her to see him frequently, maybe he asked daringly, every day. Leah blushed and a glow came to her fine eyes.

'I would like nothing better, Taylor,' she replied quietly. As he drove back to Maryport down the winding road by the sea Taylor's mind was in a conflict. Part of him reminded him that she was a married woman, yes, but an unhappy one, his brain replied. He had come so far to find her he was not going to let her go without a struggle.

Passchendaele

Passchendaele was hell made reality. A nightmarish vision so horrible it could not be imagined. A vast foetid expanse of slime, no trees, no grass, no plants, no houses or buildings of any sort, the landscape barren of living things except the miserable doomed men dying, in their thousands. The appalling conditions of this long inhuman tragedy resulted in the death and misery of over two hundred thousand men. James did not care whether he lived or died, he was indifferent to any finer feelings. He did not even desire survival. All he did was do as he was ordered. His orders were to kill. Death was all around. He did not fear it, nor did he desire it, if it came he would embrace it with the same indifference he gave to living, he could not imagine surviving, he could not imagine living. He merely lived through one hellish day to the next. He had at last received Leah's letter telling him of the death of the baby, his baby. He read it without feeling. Leah and all that was good and decent he had left in another world, a world he could not remember. The reality was Passchendaele. He had also received a letter from Mary Flanagan, telling him that she had born his daughter. He fleetingly recalled his night of passion with her, alien feelings he could not recapture, feelings from another world, a lifetime away. Mary had married an officer but he had died. She was living in England with their daughter. She made no demands of James, she simply wanted him to have the comfort of knowing that he had a child to fight for, his child who bore her husband's name. James tore up Leah's letter, the fragments sinking slowly into the muddy slime as easily as his thoughts drifted away from both women. Leah and Mary belonged to another life, a life he could not imagine anymore, a life which had happened to another person. Home was just a word, not even a feeling, not even a memory, reality was the cold and bloody mud of Passchendaele, standing in mud, eating in mud, breathing in the disgusting stench of mud, fighting in mud and ultimately moving in mud tinted thick crimson with blood. It was the ever-present rats scuttling round the parapets, and body lice. It dwindled to the telephone wire which kept them in touch with a previous world which sent them incomprehensible orders. It was dead, putrid bodies, severed limbs, men tunnelling underneath the mud like wild animals. One day, James had seen a group of tattered and shabby men with their hands tied behind their backs. Dimly he knew that they were to be shot. One he saw with a rush of pity had mutilated his hands and arms so that he could not fight. These poor frightened half-mad men, too terrified and exhausted to fight and kill any more were to be sent as an example. James turned his head away as they passed through the trenches with their firing squad to No Man's Land. Rumour had it that some of these poor wretches had been put over the top into No Man's Land, still tied together and left to their fate. James did not care. He watched them stumbling by as if watching a play. He noticed that one man, a youth, was not wearing boots and it crossed his mind to wonder where they were but the thought soon vanished and James watched dully and incuriously as they stumbled and slipped into the icy sucking mud, their faces mottled with cold and fear. One of the boys, a mere youth was crying for his Mother. James felt no sorrow, no pity.

In October, the battalion had moved by barge and road to Teteghan then near the end of November they were moved to the Belle Vue area just north of Passchendaele. That summer of 1917, there had been exceptionally heavy rainfall and ten days bombardment had destroyed the drainage system and transformed the battlefield into an impossible, impassable foul-smelling quagmire of interconnecting shell holes. The Germans were in positions they had had three years to prepare, and had constructed many concrete machine-gun posts. It was General Haig's belief that if he could defeat the Germans at Passchendaele ridge, the way into Belgium and subsequently Germany, would be clear. Months of continual shelling had blocked the water courses and the masses of shell holes frustrated every effort to drain the water away. There was no way to haul the artillery guns forward, the planks used by the engineers floated away or sank in the mire, the dugouts and trenches were flooded. With men unable to repair them, many of the guns had sunk up to their muzzles in the mud. James drew the utterly hopeless scenes in his notebook. Somehow by drawing the horrors which unfolded each day, he could psychologically distance himself from them as if he saw reality through a dark curtain. He drew the flooded trenches and dugouts where men were surviving like pursued animals day by day. He drew the battle weary, brain dead soldiers, most of them just young boys, standing in the muddy water waiting for night to come when ammunitions and food were carried to them through the mud. He drew the lifeline of the telephone wire, in his head he heard the continuing litany 'Watch the wire. Watch the wire.' He drew the pitiful wrecks of men who had been gassed, coughing out their life's blood from ragged perforated lungs. He drew the mutilated and the dying and the men gone mad; by drawing the horror, he made it unreal. One day in amazement he seemed to watch himself as if he was a stranger, drawing a badly wounded man drowning in the mud and he realised dimly that he had lost any feelings of compassion or sorrow. He drew the drowned bodies of the dead and abandoned, he drew the wounded and all the time he drew the almost unrecognisable fragments of bodies. And still he survived. Kill or be killed.

In December, the battalion was ordered to take part in a night attack on the German positions. James lay on his back in the freezing water and mud. Around him men lay silent waiting for zero hour. The dark was impenetrable until the sky was lit up by the barrage beginning. James rose from the mud with his ghost-like companions. A great wave of shrieking, howling humanity, they tried to race through the clinging mud to the German positions whilst all the time the German machine-gunners methodically raked death in swathes of men. James ran forward and gaining the German defences drew his bayonet. He knew not how many men he killed, a red mist swirled before his eyes and he stabbed and gouged and killed in an orgy of despair. One young German scarcely more than a boy, stretched out his hand to James in a gesture of supplication but James unheeding, a deathly automaton, pierced the boy's side with his bayonet and with a disgusting satisfaction twisted the murderous point again and again so that the young boy screamed in agony. At last he felt something but the feeling was blood lust and a revolting desire to inflict pain on the young boy as if to make him atone for the months of despair and grief he had endured. After he had killed the young boy, so slowly that he begged to die, James felt nothing, no fear, no pity, no shame, no remorse, he was the living dead as all around him men slaughtered and died and screamed and cursed. The day was endless and when night came, they were forced to give up their hard won positions and retreat. James slithered and clawed his way back to the lines. He clambered over dead and dying men, drowning in the mud, the stain of murdered blood had spread through the mud in great rusty globules and he slid in the bloody stained bath and clawed his way through it, ignoring the pitiful cries of the wounded begging for help, his body determined to survive but his mind shielding him from the ghastly sights and sounds. James lived through Passchendaele. He was one of the 'lucky ones'… but he was no longer human. He had become a killing machine as devoid of emotion as the ceaseless pounding guns.

Love

Taylor stayed as long as he felt he could leave his business. He had given himself time to get to know Leah. If, he thought, he could not, did not, care for her, he would only stay a little while he assured himself. Yet in his heart of hearts he knew that he was more than a little in love with Leah already. In the event he stayed five weeks until he felt he must return to his business. It was the longest time he had ever neglected his business but he did not regret a day. He saw Leah every day, and every day was not long enough for him. He had loved her through her letters and now he loved her as a person with whom he felt he could spend the rest of his life. Sometimes he took her out in his car. Leah had travelled only in necessity in her life and he brought her own beautiful county to life. He took her to the bustling little town of Keswick and they walked beside Lake Derwent Water to Friar's Crag and surveyed the beautiful scenery. Taylor insisted that he and Leah had their photograph taken together at Abraham's the photographers. When she received it by post two weeks later, she was stunned at how happy and how right they looked together, their fair heads drawn together in mutual affection. He took her to the little market town of Penrith and to many little villages near the beautiful lakes and mountains which had lain undiscovered till Wordsworth's verse had made them famous. Leah enjoyed seeing the beautiful sights of her birthland but most of all, Leah liked it best when they walked beside the Solway and just talked. They walked whatever the weather and always seemed to find much to say. Taylor had the vitality of his race.

'You see, Leah,' he explained, 'in my country, anyone can be anything. There are no rules of class or inherited wealth. If you strive, you succeed and life is there for the taking.'

One day, Leah found herself laughing uproariously at a joke Taylor had made. She stopped and looked at him seriously.

'It is so long since I laughed,' she admitted. He turned his bright blue gaze upon her.

'Your life should be full of laughter, Leah,' he said warmly, 'you have seen too much sorrow already in your young life.'

Leah felt herself grow young again, she felt life returning to her. Each morning, anticipating Taylor's arrival, she felt a tingle of anticipation. Each day she chose her clothes with care, did up her pale blonde hair carefully. It was the first time since the baby's death that she had greeted the day with a smile and every day was precious. She had missed talking, Billy and she had talked about everything under the sun and they had educated each other. She had also missed a man's attention and Taylor's attention and unspoken affection made her bloom again. Taylor's conversations were bright and sparkling and roused her, almost challenged her to follow his wide-ranging interests. He told her about Boston, the windy little city enclosed in its blue harbour with its jumble of historic houses and memories of the revolution against the British. He told her of New York, of its vitality as the melting pot of a new nation. She could imagine the Statue of Liberty, donated by the French to commemorate America's revolution against the British, standing proud, welcoming the poor and oppressed with a beckoning arm. She could imagine the immigrants, some with no more than a suitcase, chased from their homes by this vile war, seeing the statue for the first time, a symbol of freedom, knowing whatever their race or creed they were welcome.

'I remember,' she said slowly, 'when you were at the Hall, you prophesised to the Captain that the old order would be swept away.'

There was a pause as they both remembered the conversation. Taylor broke the silence.

'It is, Leah,' he said vehemently.

'Change is all around you, even in somewhere as secluded as Cumberland. Europe is dying. It is killing itself. Who will govern England when this War is over? The flower of youth is being systematically annihilated. Day after day the slaughter goes on and who will be left?'

Leah shuddered. Who indeed? She thought of Billy, beautiful Billy, cut down in his prime, the backbone of England. She thought of James, his artistic sensitivity, his fine spirit, killing his fellow men and her face clouded. Taylor, ever sensitive to her mood, guessed at her thoughts.

'Leah,' he asked, greatly daring, 'are you in love with James?'

Leah looked at him, her cool grey eyes misting over. She knew instinctively that her future hinged on her reply. There was a long silence as she thought how to phrase her reply.

'I have always been truthful to you, Taylor,' she said her voice husky with emotion, 'when I wrote to you it was as if,' she paused and said shyly, 'to my dearest friend.'

Taylor looked at her, hardly daring to imagine what she would say next.

'I don't love James,' she faltered, 'I was lonely. You cannot imagine how lonely I was up on the fells...' she burst out, her voice breaking.

'...and he took advantage of that loneliness,' Taylor growled in contempt.

'No, Taylor,' Leah replied firmly, 'we took advantage of each other's loneliness and despair.' She stopped, thinking of James and their wild lovemaking.

'If I had not been pregnant maybe things would have been different. No,' she put up her hand to prevent Taylor from speaking. 'It happened and I am married. For good or ill. I am a married woman.' She turned her face away from him so that he could not see the look of anguish in her face or the tears welling from her eyes. Taylor put his hand on her shoulder.

'I am, would like to be, still your dearest friend, Leah,' he said gently, fearful that she might sever their relationship, knowing that, on whatever terms, he wanted to keep her in his life, to know of her welfare. He knew that she did not love James and his heart sang. Who knew what would happen in this dreadful war? So many had not returned.

He pushed the thought away from him, knowing that whatever he wished, he did not want Leah to suffer again.

One day they went to visit Flora who was now living in a small house in Workington. The Hall had proved too full of ghosts for her to remain. Taylor was shocked to see how reduced in life the once proud Flora was. He spoke to her gently and towards the end of their visit made her laugh and a flush came to her cheeks and the brown eyes glowed reminding them of her once proud looks.

'I am pleased to see you, Taylor,' Flora said when they were leaving, 'for I am deeply ashamed still of the circumstances which made you leave the Hall so angrily.'

Taylor took her hand.

'Flora,' he said quietly, 'things like that will never happen again.' He did not mention Flora's Mother or talk about the Hall for Leah had told him of Mrs Forbes Robertson's death and the decay of the once beautiful Netherghyll Hall.

'Flora and I have become friends now,' said Leah, 'we have a shared history.'

'And a shared family, too,' said Flora quietly. The thought of James hung unspoken in the tiny room and there was silence until Flora said thoughtfully, 'How strange that after all these awful years you should return and we have all met again. James will be astounded when he knows.'

She and Leah discussed the fact that they had not heard from James for over a month although this was not unusual in war time. Taylor was perturbed by the conversation and did not want to think of Leah and James together in any context, however he managed to behave with great civility and he took leave of Flora as if leaving a friend.

They did not talk about personal matters until a few days before his departure. The rain had swept in over the Solway, the sky was flat and grey, the white edges of the waves dashing and splattering over the green turf as they walked. Now they sat in the little parlour, the firelight sparkling on the copper, the curtains drawn against the darkness. Will and Lucy had long retired but it was as if neither could end the day and say goodnight to each other. They sat for a long time unspeaking, each deep in their own thoughts, dreading their separation yet knowing that one word would declare what they felt and it would be best unspoken. Taylor spoke softly into the silence.

'You know, you must know that I love you, Leah,' he said, feeling that he could not put thousands of miles between them and not say what was in his heart. He looked at Leah. A flush rose subtly in her pale checks, her eyes were huge and luminous. He desired her more than anything he had ever wanted in his life.

'I want you to be my wife.'

He had not intended to say the words but they burst from him uncontrollably. Leah gasped. She stayed silent for all her instincts clamoured for her to follow his declaration, yet the thought of James and her sacred vow of marriage made her hesitate. Taylor took her hand in his two hands, holding it as if he would never let her go.

'I need to know, Leah. I do not want to return to America not knowing your feelings. If you feel nothing for me,' he burst out with passion, 'at least I will know my fate.'

Leah looked at him, her grey eyes burning, 'I am a married woman, Taylor,' she whispered, 'and not free to love you. But,' she paused as Taylor held his breath, 'if I were free to love, my answer would be that I love you. That I would be honoured to be your wife.' There was a long silence. They looked at each other, grey eyes met blue and seemed to melt in each other. Taylor felt a tide of passion rising in him which he could not deny.

'Leah,' he cried with longing, 'Leah.' Slowly, so slowly he pulled her into his arms and very softly placed his lips on hers, gently at first and then with an unbearable hunger until he had pulled her body close to his and she could feel his blood pounding in his body and the fresh aromatic smell of him in her nostrils. All the passion that she had repressed, all the desperate need she had subdued since her lovemaking with James overwhelmed her and she allowed Taylor to gently pull her close to him on the rug in front of the fire. He pulled out the pins in her hair and buried his face in the sweetness. She held him close hungering for his body. His hands fumbled urgently at the small buttons at her neck and then he ripped open the fastening and her breasts, unfettered, tumbled sweetly into his hands. He bent his head to kiss them, God but she was gorgeous. The pale globes of her breasts felt cool under his fiery lips and he took the large pink nipples into his mouth and rolled them with his eager tongue. He pulled up her skirts and his hand felt for the moist secret place between her long smooth legs. His fingers were urgent and he felt her swift arousal like swelling silk, Leah was drowning in her senses. Taylor's kiss had unlocked her body and all her being clamoured for his caresses. His fingers spread her and caressed her and urged her on, and with a shudder she climaxed, her orgasm intense and sweet. She lay in his arms shaking as he touched her again.

'I want you, Leah,' he murmured, 'I want you. Be mine. Give yourself to me.'

His mouth clasped her nipple and his fingers touched her so subtly and so sweetly that her body moved urgently of its own accord against his searching fingers and after long moments when she clung to him and moved against him, lost of all control once again she shuddered, moving against him without restraint, feeling only his touch, moaning his name over and over again. Taylor looked down at her, at her face suffused with emotion, feeling her completely his in his arms, his to do with whatever he wanted and he felt a great wave of love sweep over him. It would be so easy to enter her, to take her, to put his imprint on her, to make her smell of lust, the cloying heady smell of sex, but he knew that he did not want her like that. He knew that she would bitterly regret any physical completeness with him and that in her guilt afterwards he might lose her. He held her gently like a child, soothing her, stroking the wonderful pale hair until his own desire ebbed and at last she lay supine in his arms. The flushed cheeks had cooled and her grey eyes were closed from his gaze.

'I love you, Leah,' he murmured huskily, 'I love you.' Her eyes opened, fringed by the long dark lashes.

'I love you, Taylor,' she whispered brokenly and hooked her hand around his neck to pull his lips close to hers once more.

They parted very formally, the next day. Will cried and demanded kisses and Lucy covered her eyes with her apron for she had taken a fancy to Taylor and felt the unspoken love between him and her mistress and it touched her romantic soul. He took her hand in his and placed it to his lips.

'Write to me soon, Leah' he said soberly, 'I will come as soon as you call.'

Leah's eyes filled with tears and her voice trembled.

'I will write soon. Goodbye my... dearest friend.'

She watched as the car turned the corner of the winding road. The day was grey and melancholy to match her mood and a fine drizzle driven by a shrill wind veiled her hair. She stood for a long time until at last she went back into the cottage and closed the door.

Return

Leah stood nervously an the platform under the sooty arches of the Citadel station. Only four weeks after Taylor's departure, she had received a frantic phone call from Flora.

'James has wired me that he is returning home. He has asked that you meet him.'

'Why has he not asked me himself?' Leah asked in surprise although in her heart she knew the answer.

'Maybe,' replied Flora slowly, 'he is unsure of a welcome.' She thought of Taylor and the obvious affection between him and Leah and felt a pang of something like pain. How she wished that she had someone to love her.

'Of course I will meet him,' said Leah firmly, 'if that is what he wishes.'

She had read of the dreadful battle of Passchendaele and her feelings for James were a mixture of pity and shame that she could have a glimpse of happiness with Taylor whilst he endured unimaginable horrors.

'I will meet him at Carlisle. Tell me when.'

And so she stood, her heart beating like a wild thing, waiting to meet the husband she hardly remembered. The train with a screech and groan pulled noisily into the station and gusts of black smoke filled the atmosphere rendering Leah unable to see through its gritty blackness. When the smoke cleared she could have screamed aloud. Further up the platform, unmoving, stood James, at least she thought it was James. Only the auburn hair straggling from underneath his cap gave her a clue that it might be he. She walked slowly towards him, this man who had returned from the War, hoping it was not him yet knowing with an awful truth that it was. James. He stood perfectly still as she approached. He was painfully, tortuously slender, his shoulders stooped as if with great fatigue. She noticed that he supported his right leg with a stick and remembered in a flash of shame the wounds she had kissed so long ago on the Caldbeck Fells. But it was his eyes which riveted her attention. His hazel eyes, once so warm and lively were flat and lifeless, devoid of all feeling, the eyes of a man who had been to hell and had returned.

'James,' she moved towards him timidly and laid a hand on the rough material of his uniform. He looked at her unspeaking, unsmiling.

'Leah,' his voice was a breath, a rasp, before a fit of coughing overtook him and he turned his head away in a paroxysm of distress. Leah felt her heart move with pity at the sight. This wreck of a once young and vibrant man moved her immensely and tears came to her eyes. When he had finished coughing she took him gently by the hand.

'Come, James,' she said softly and led him over the bridge to where the train to Maryport was waiting. Silently, James walked beside her, he could hardly believe that he was home, did not really care. They got into the carriage and sat opposite each other. James looked at her.

'I'm sorry, Leah,' he said tiredly, 'I had nowhere else to go. No one to come home to.' His eyes closed and his head flopped back against the seat in exhaustion.

'It's all right, James,' said Leah steadily, 'I'm taking you home.'

He smiled but did not open his eyes. As the train puffed and panted and stopped and started in the little oil lit country stations, Leah studied James. His face had an unhealthy pallor and there were deep lines of suffering cleaving his cheeks. His hair had no shine and lay flat to his well-shaped head. All the time he slept, he clutched his haversack as if he would never let it go. He looked immeasurably old. Her husband. She thought of Taylor. He had known no war, no privations. She knew that she loved him, that she would always love him for his spirit and energy and intelligence and that the man opposite her was no more than a stranger, but she thought of Billy and what it would have been like if he had returned to her from this ghastly War and she knew where her duty lay. This man had endured so much. How could she cast him out, tell him she loved another man? She had born his child. He was her husband. She set her mouth firmly. This was where her duty lay. James opened his eyes once during the long journey. He looked at her in surprise and said in a wondering voice 'Leah.'

Then he closed his eyes again as another fit of coughing overcame him. There was a car waiting for them at the echoing Maryport station and soon they were in the little cottage by the sea where the bright lights burned and a fire was lit in the hearth. As they had made the journey along the coast, Leah had told him about the cottage and how happy she was there.

'You will be peaceful there, James,' she said quietly, 'you can rest there until you recover.' James heard her voice as if from a long way off. Peace? What was that? Quiet? The pounding of the guns and the shrieks of the dying still echoed in his weary head. He was silent. James sank down in one of the green velvet armchairs. It all seemed so unreal. He had lived with death and killing too long, they were more real to him than life. Lucy, the little maid could not help giving an exclamation of pity when she saw James, then she bustled away to bring a warming cup of tea and a piece of home-made cake. James could barely speak and very soon mounted the stairs to bed. Leah had moved Will to the top floor room opposite Lucy and had had his room made ready for James. A fire burned in the little grate and the oil lamp was lit ready. The bed was turned down and a stone hot water bottle warmed the crisp sheets. James turned to look at Leah.

'Thank you,' he said simply. It was such a wonderful sight to James, so normal yet so extraordinary that he lost control and tears slipped down his sunken cheeks. Leah turned away in distress, immeasurably moved and bade him goodnight. She went back down to the parlour and sat in front of the blazing fire. James's haversack lay on the carpet. On an impulse she opened it. It contained a few items of clothing but mainly its contents were sketchbooks and exercise books. Overcome with curiosity, Leah opened one. Her hand shook in horror as she turned the leaves and saw the war caught in all its brutality in James's pictures. She was revolted by the drawings but she could not stop looking and as she did she felt a horrible shame at the sights she saw. How could James, how could anyone, survive such carnage? The pictures leapt off the page in their brutal honesty and moved her so much she began to cry in pity. The last sketchbook was bound in Morocco leather and was very worn. She opened it and there were pictures of the Hall as it had been so many innocent years before. Mrs Forbes Robertson stared at her from the page with a proud uncompromising gaze and there was a much younger Flora. She idled over the book and just as she was about to return it a folded piece of paper fell out from between the covers. She picked it up and opened it. It was the drawing James had made of her at the pool and her naked image was so beautiful, so innocent, that she gazed at it a long time. James had written on the bottom.

'My dream.'

Slowly she replaced the books in the haversack. A crumpled envelope caught her eye in the very bottom. Slowly she opened the torn flap and took out the letter to

James which Mary Flanagan had written telling him news of his daughter. A daughter. She thought of her own child which had died. James had a daughter and she had no child to hold. She felt no jealousy for the other woman, no curiosity, no pity.

Wearily Leah replaced the letter. How long ago it was. She thought of Billy and Taylor who she would love for ever and she thought of James, poor damaged James. She lay that night in the room opposite, listening to his uneasy sleep, his tortured cough, his moans, and steely eyed she was determined that she would look after James as he deserved. She would grow to love him, she vowed with all her heart.

Illness

James was desperately ill for several days. His temperature rose until his gaunt emaciated body was bathed in sweat as a high fever overcame him. It was as if the self-control which had enabled him to survive the horrors he had endured had deserted him and left him naked to the nightmares he had lived through. He shook uncontrollably and sometimes cried in a heartbreakingly simple way, tears falling in great waves down his hollow cheeks as he gulped the air. Sometimes he called out in his delirium, hoarsely exhorting his invisible companions to rise up over the parapets and, 'Kill the bastards.'

Sometimes too, he swore foul oaths and railed against God whilst sometimes he shrank into the bed in a foetal position trying to cover his head with the bedclothes in his terror. Sometimes, more frightening still, his poor tortured body mimicked the killing and he rose up out of the sweat stained sheets his actions terrible to see. And all the time he coughed, great tearing coughs which seemed to be about to rip his lungs apart and burst open his chest. Leah sent for the little doctor from Maryport and watched silently as he examined James, listening to his heart and his poor tortured lungs spurting out great gasps for air. There was a livid burn on James's thin chest to which the doctor paid great attention. The doctor administered a sedative to James and when he had quieted somewhat, he gestured to Leah to leave the room, his face grave. He followed Leah into the bright little sitting room and looking at her enquiring face, shook his head sadly.

'He is very ill, Mrs Forbes Robertson. I fear the gas has done irreparable damage to his lungs.'

'Gas,' cried Leah aghast, 'what gas?'

'My dear,' the doctor answered gently, 'the Germans have been using mustard gas on our brave soldiers.'

'Mustard gas?' Leah repeated in horror. 'They have used gas?' she repeated dazedly.

'Yes, my dear,' the little doctor answered sadly, his face sombre with pain.

'How can this be true?' demanded Leah wildly. 'It can't be true. Men cannot do this to each other.'

The doctor took her hands gently.

'I know because my son has told me,' he replied quietly, 'he is a doctor at the front. He has been home on leave only recently.'

His voice shook as he spoke.

'One day some soldiers arrived. Their faces were grey and their lips were blue. Their eyes were bulging out of their heads and the veins in their temples thick and grey.' He paused. 'They tore at their chests as if they would tear their hearts out of their bodies. The Germans had come in gas masks and gassed their friends. Thousands died a horrible death as they stood in the trenches, a yellow fog enveloping them. The men who arrived had tried to outrun the gas but they were too late.'

He stopped and covered his face and continued in a muffled voice when he had recovered himself a little.

'Greenish yellow spittle and froth was coming from their mouths. There was nothing my son could do for them, God rest their souls, they died a horrible death.'

The enormity of what she had heard slowly penetrated Leah's brain.

'How could they do this?' she begged wildly, 'Gas people? This war, this horrible, evil war,' she sobbed wildly.

The little doctor waited until her sobs died down.

'I am sorry, my dear, to tell you of such outrage but in the circumstances I had no choice.'

'No choice?' Leah repeated numbly, 'What do you mean in the circumstances?'

'Sit down, my dear,' the doctor replied compassionately, and when she had done so, he took her hand again and said sadly, 'There is no hope for your husband, Mrs Forbes Robertson. The gas has irreparably damaged his lungs. I know that you saw the burn on his chest, that too was the result of the gas.'

'No hope?' cried Leah, 'What do you mean?' she demanded incredulously.

'I mean,' continued the doctor gravely, 'that to put it at its simplest, your husband's body is not strong enough to withstand the effects of the gas in his lungs, it is as if he were suffering the last stages of tuberculosis, only for this there is no possible cure.'

Leah looked at him, the blood draining from her face, she could feel her body begin to tremble and the room darken slowly as the implications of what the doctor had said entered her shocked brain. She shook her head dazedly and the mist cleared.

'I knew he was ill,' she faltered, 'but not this. Not this obscene thing,' she shuddered uncontrollably.

'He is very ill, my dear,' the doctor interrupted, 'mortally ill.'

Leah turned her white face to him and said pitifully, 'How long?'

'I cannot tell,' the doctor replied, 'it may be sooner than later or it could be years instead of months. All I can tell you is that he is gravely ill and all you can do is make him as comfortable as possible. I will help you all I can,' he added gently, 'I will treat him as if he were my own son.

'Will he know?' asked Leah.

The doctor smiled at her sadly, 'Only if you choose to tell him, my dear. It is up to you.'

Leah sat numbly in the bright room after the doctor had gone. Her heart was torn with pity and sorrow. She thought of James as the sensitive boy she had known years before, before this dreadful war had ruined him. She thought of his sensitive face and his chestnut hair and the bright hazel eyes. Lizzie and she, in the little attic room, had pitied him his life with the overbearing Mrs Forbes Robertson. He had had no life, no young man's dreams, no fun, no love. She thought of Taylor whom she loved with all her heart and her face hardened. Taylor was thousands of miles away from this ghastly war knowing nothing of the suffering and the dreadful waste. She thought of Billy, sweet Billy, who she had loved as a young girl. Well, the girl was a woman now. She would not fail James, however long it took, she would care for him, make him comfortable, love him as much as she could. She thought of the ardent young man on the Caldbeck Fells, already marked by war and remembered their lovemaking under the wide blue sky. She had thought that nothing worse could have happened after she had lost her child, but this, this was an even greater horror. She must be strong for James's sake. That night, she sat at her little desk and wrote to Taylor O'Neill. She started the letter, *My dearest friend…* and as she had done so many times before, she wrote about her life. She told him of the decision she had made and finished *Do not write to me. Let it be as it was before…*

James lay in the soft bed listening to the sounds of the household stirring. It was so peaceful. He could hear the sounds of the sea shushing in the background and a pale sun was fingering its way through the open curtains. A soft breeze was moving them and he lay and watched them shiver and shake in the draught. The curtains were always open, as he feared the dark as he feared the night when the horrors of war returned to his tired brain. How peaceful it was. How much he loved Leah. She had cared for him through the worst of his fever, washed him gently, fed him carefully, so gently, so sweetly, her lovely face intent as she ministered to him. It seemed impossible to believe that she could care for him. No, he thought, she was just sorry for him and yet he dared to hope that one day she would love him, dammit, he would make her love him. A bout of coughing interrupted his train of thought and he sank back against the pillows defeated in his weakness.

The doctor from Maryport made frequent visits. He felt a compassion for James compounded by thoughts of his own dear son. One day in early summer he told a delighted James that he could come downstairs for a short period of time and then when he felt well enough he could venture outside. Leah sat with James each afternoon, sometimes talking, sometimes silent. Flora had been to see James several times, making the long train and bus journey. The brother and sister had grown closer on these visits although James did not wish to talk about the Hall. Flora's husband was shortly to return after recuperation and they would move back to the chandler's shop in Whitehaven. James was moved by the change in his once proud sister, just as she was moved by how weak James was.

'James,' Leah said to him suddenly one afternoon, 'when you are feeling a little stronger, would you like to visit the Hall? Wilson would send his car for us, I know.'

James was silent for so long that Leah felt she had made a mistake in asking him and was unprepared for his answer.

'Yes, Leah,' he said slowly, 'I would like to see it, to visit it. To say goodbye to it.'

The unexpectedness of the answer astonished Leah, 'To say goodbye?' she repeated.

'I was never happy there, Leah,' James said sombrely, 'it is part of my past. A past which has gone for ever. I cannot return to the life I had then, everything has been blown away, the old days are gone.'

Leah thought of Taylor's comment so many years ago, how true it was. The War had changed so many lives, so many things taken for granted.

'Sometime, when I am well,' James continued, 'we must think of our future! I must get my affairs in order.'

Leah felt a wave of sadness sweep over her. How long a future would James have. True, he was making progress and seemed stronger but, she looked at him keenly, his face was still drawn with suffering and there were streaks of grey in the auburn hair. She knew that the nightmares continued for she could hear James each night in the grip of the horrors he could not erase. She smiled gently at him.

'There will be time enough when you are well, James,' she said comfortably.

'Just keep on getting a little stronger each day. Maybe,' she said with a stroke of inspiration, 'we could buy a car when you are better.'

James's face lit up with enthusiasm and his face looked boyish for a brief moment.

'Oh, I should like that, Leah,' he replied animatedly, 'that would be wonderful.'

Each day, they sat and talked and each day they knew each other a little better. As the weather got warmer, James seemed to be a little stronger although the dreadful cough still wracked his body. On the warmest of days, he had taken to sitting in the little forecourt garden in a comfortable chair, covered in a rug and gazing contentedly at the sea. The doctor did not come so frequently now and Leah began to hope that his prediction had been a mistake.

James's pale face took a little colour and his hair began to recover a shine. He passed the time of day with the villagers, many of who had sons in the war or had lost sons in the war and he basked in the feeling of being a local hero. One day, as Leah came out to sit with him he caught hold of her hand.

'You have made me very happy, Leah,' he said quietly, 'I thank you from the bottom of my heart.'

He looked up at her. She was wearing a simple grey cotton dress which accentuated the colour of her lovely eyes. Her glorious hair was in a loose chignon at her neck. He looked at her slim body longingly, yet he felt no physical yearning for her, those thoughts belonged to another time, another place long ago in his life, yet still he thought she was the loveliest creature he had ever seen. Leah let her hand lie in his for a long moment and something deep inside her impelled her to say, 'You have made me happy too, James.'

They looked at each other for a long moment and they smiled easily at each other.

'We are two damaged people, Leah,' James said softly. 'Fate has brought us together in a strange way has it not?'

Leah nodded slowly in agreement. Yes, they had both been damaged. She thought of Billy, her lovely Billy, lying in a French cemetery far from his beloved fells and sighed a deep sigh.

'You are thinking of Billy,' James said perceptively. Leah had not expected such a comment. She stiffened and then relaxed.

'Yes, James,' she replied truthfully, 'I loved him very much.'

James stared at the sea. He wanted to tell her of his love for her, of how he felt he could not live without her, beg her not to leave him, tell her he could not imagine life without her, but he was silent. They were man and wife, they would have time he hoped. Leah broke the silence.

'James,' she said, 'there is something I must ask you. Something which upset me deeply,' she paused as James looked at her questioningly, 'you have a lock of my hair which I gave to Billy,' she stopped, unable to continue. James understood the unspoken question immediately.

'I will tell you how I come to have it, Leah,' he replied, 'I fear it will upset you.'

Quietly he told her of Billy's death and how the lock of hair in its golden clasp had fallen from Billy's hand as he fell dying.

'It was like a talisman on that field of death, Leah,' he faltered, 'a symbol of brightness and gentleness. I know I should have returned it to you with Billy's possessions but I felt possessing it would somehow keep me safe.'

'Oh, James,' cried Leah, her face full of sorrow and pity, 'if only you had told me. I wondered so many times.'

'You thought I had taken it off Billy's dead body,' James said slowly. She turned away, ashamed, touched at his revelation.

Gradually their conversations became more intimate. She told him of Taylor's visit, hoping that the words she chose and her face would not betray her deep feelings for him. She told James of the many letters she had sent to Taylor and of the shock of seeing him in the flesh. As she spoke, she could picture the moment when she turned and saw Taylor looking down at her, his bright blue eyes smiling into hers and she had a piercing longing to see him, to hold him to tell him that she loved him. Her voice trailed away.

'I always liked him,' said James into the silence, 'when you write to him again please convey my regards.'

Leah sat silent. She remembered Taylor taking her hand as they sat in the little parlour and she remembered with an aching heart the loss of her baby, James's baby.

'I wanted to die when I lost the baby,' she said wearily. It was the first time she had mentioned it at all.

'I wanted her so much,' she said softly, 'a child to hold, something to love in the middle of all this carnage and confusion. When I knew I was pregnant, I wished her dead but then as I began to feel her grow inside me, I longed for her...' she began to cry.

'Hush, Leah,' James whispered pitifully.

'Hush. Please don't cry.' His own eyes filled with tears and his voice shook with weakness, 'Please don't cry.'

Leah moved towards him and knelt beside him. She put her arms round his thin shoulders and bent her head against his chest. James sat quite still, then wonderingly he put out his shaking hand and stroked her hair gently. The gentleness of his touch moved Leah's heart and for a long time they sat close together, united in their sorrow. That night, when James cried out fretfully in his sleep, Leah slipped out of bed, crossed the little corridor and entered his room. The lamp was turned down low, for James was still unable to endure the darkness and she stood and looked at him for a long moment. How ill he looked, how pale. Decisively she lifted the bedclothes and slipped in beside him. She put her arms round him as she would to Will when he came running with some hurt and held him close to her as a Mother with a baby.

'Hush,' she murmured, 'hush. It's all right. There is nothing here to hurt you.'

James roused at her voice and touch.

'Oh, Leah,' he murmured as he relaxed in her arms, 'I love you.' Leah held him close to her, feeling the fragile, thin body of a once young man, conscious of his heart pounding beneath the thin ribs. Tears came to her eyes and she held him close.

'Hush James,' she whispered, 'hush. I'm here.'

She lay a long time before sleep overcame her, thinking of the fate which had shaped her destiny, of Billy whom she had loved as a young girl, of Taylor who had captured her heart, and James who she had grown to love as a Mother loves a child. She held him close to her heart. If she could make him happy she vowed to herself, she would. She would do all in her power to heal him. She put away the thought of death. There had been too much in her life already. As the clear light of dawn touched the window, she fell asleep at last, lulled by the sound of the sea and the beating of James's heart close against her breast.

The End

James died the week before the Armistice was declared. He had seemed to be recovering during the long summer months and Leah's spirits rose and she began to believe that the doctor's prediction had been wrong. However, as autumn closed in and the days got longer, James's mood became sombre and his desire to live diminished. The cough which had alleviated returned and one day, in the bright parlour, after James had coughed up a spurt of terrifying crimson blood along with the yellow slime, the little doctor shook his head and said wearily to Leah, 'He is slipping away from us, Leah, I fear it will not be long.'

He took her hand gently in his, 'It will be kinder for him, my dear.'

His only son, the doctor, had written to him to say that he was returning from the front and he felt, despite a great happiness at the news, an overwhelming feeling of sadness for James, as if it were his son who was dying. Leah turned her head away, her grey eyes full of tears, she struggled to speak.

'Yes. I do know that,' she said softly, 'but it is so… unfair.' She had learned to love James in his helplessness and in a strange way caring for him had made her feel as if she were caring for Billy and coming to terms with losing him. She spent many nights just holding James close, gently as if she held a child, calming him in his nightmares.

'He could have lived many years and suffered dreadfully,' the little doctor said suddenly, 'you must let him go, my dear, and thank God that he has not to spend his life in pain.'

Leah was silent. She could not reconcile those sort of feelings in her heart.

Soon, James spent all his time in bed; he ceased to want to live as memories of the War became more real to him than his day-to-day existence in the quiet little house. He visited the trenches in his daylight hours, smelled the smell of death, and relived the indelible images of the horrors he had been a part of. Leah spent most of her time in his room, reading or sewing or seeing to his needs. Will, too, like a little animal needing reassurance brought his toys in and seemed instinctively to know not to make a noise. He had formed an attachment with James whilst he had been well and lingered near him now.

One cold grey autumn afternoon, with the wind lashing rain on to the windows, Leah sat looking into the flames of the fire lit in the little cast iron grate. James had been restless during the night and had twice tried to climb out of the bed where Leah held him close. Tears of pain and exhaustion rolled unchecked down her cheeks. She cried for James and Billy and the hideous war which had deprived so many men of a life. She turned to the bed and became aware of James watching her, his hazel eyes bright in his gaunt face.

'Don't cry, Leah,' he whispered, his voice rasping and uneven. Quickly, she went to him and held his hand.

'I'm not afraid to die, Leah,' he murmured so softly she could hardly hear, 'I have died so many times already and seen so many die. I am so tired.' He gave a great sigh and closed his eyes and turned his head away. It was many minutes before Leah realised that he was dead. Under his pillow was the lock of Leah's hair in its golden clasp.

★

James was buried in the Forbes Robertson family vault at the Church at Ghyllside. There were few mourners and those who were there came out of respect to the family. Leah had expected somehow that the village would be changed but the only change was that Wilson Beck's little shop had been replaced by a new Co-operative. Three miles up the road, Netherghyll Hall stood shuttered and empty, the echoing dusty rooms still as they used to be, the furniture shrouded, the bells silent. Leah, now the owner of the Hall and after discussion with Flora and her husband, had put it up for sale. However, no one wanted this relic from a past gone for ever. Times had changed never to return. The scandal of the young master and the servant girl was long forgotten. People had lived through too many years of pain and somehow the old ways were no longer important. Peace and the problems which it would bring was only days away, yet people were tired and bruised. Leah stood silently beside Flora and her husband as the vault was sealed. Wilson Beck and her Mother stood at one side of her and Flora and her husband on the other.

'You made him happy,' Flora said softly, 'he loved you very much.'

'And I loved him in return,' Leah replied. For it was true. She had not loved James with the passion and innocence with which she had loved Billy or with the maturity and recognition with which she loved Taylor but she had loved James for his courage and his dignity.

The little cottage seemed empty at first and it was hard for Leah to return to a life without James. The days seemed empty and meaningless. Leah wrote to Mary Flanagan who had born James's child, telling her of his death. She received a warm reply which was the beginning of a long and close correspondence and a photograph of the little girl, Lydia, her dark eyes a haunting echo of James. During the winter months Leah grieved. She grieved for Billy and the life she might have had as his beloved wife living a natural span and she grieved for James and his short and pain-filled life. She had suffered so much in the past few years and the world had changed to a more dangerous and unfamiliar place. It was spring before she wrote to Taylor. A fresh clean sunshine filled the room with a promise of a new beginning. She felt for the first time a desire to live her life, to be free of the ghosts and shadows.

'You are only a young woman,' Leah's Mother had said to her at their last meeting, 'you have a life in front of you. The past, sad as it is, is past.'

Leah had no doubts that Taylor loved her, that she only had to call and he would be there with his warming, glorious love. She smiled to herself as she picked up her pen.

My dearest friend, she wrote. She stopped and looked at the words for a long time then decisively she crossed out the words and wrote, *My darling Taylor...*